P9-DVK-394

ALSO BY GERALD PETIEVICH

Money-Men
One-Shot Deal
To Die in Beverly Hills
To Live and Die in L.A.
The Quality of the Informant

SHAKE

NEW YORK · LONDON · TORONTO · SYDNEY · TOKYO

erald Petievich

DOWN

SIMON AND SCHUSTER

Copyright © 1988 by Gerald Petievich
All rights reserved
including the right of reproduction
in whole or in part in any form.
Published by Simon and Schuster
A Division of Simon & Schuster, Inc.
Simon & Schuster Building
Rockefeller Center
1230 Avenue of the Americas
New York, NY 10020
SIMON AND SCHUSTER and colophon are
registered trademarks of Simon & Schuster, Inc.
Manufactured in the United States of America

10 9 8 7 6 5 4 3 2 1

Library of Congress Cataloging in Publication Data

Petievich, Gerald.
  Shakedown

  I. Title.
PS3566.E773S53 1988   813'.54   87-23419
ISBN 0-671-63154-3

SHAKEDOWN

1 Rodeo Drive was crowded with limousines and luxury cars double-parked in front of shops with foreign names. The sidewalks, runways for a parade of fashionably dressed and coiffed lady shoppers, had a scrubbed look, unlike the grimy, booze-stained pavements of downtown Las Vegas that Eddie Sands knew so well.

Finally, Sands spotted a pay telephone. He swerved the brown four-door sedan to the curb. Though it was the middle of a heat wave, he shrugged on his suit jacket before climbing out of the air-conditioned car. He did this to shield the revolver, handcuffs, and bullet pouch on his belt. Standing at the curb in the ovenlike heat, he rummaged through his pockets for change. He had none.

He entered the nearest establishment, the Beverly

Rodeo Hotel; in the gift shop, he handed a twenty-dollar bill to a blond woman behind the counter and asked for change. The woman gave him a cold Beverly Hills smile and punched a cash-register key. As she plucked coins and bills from the drawer, Sands surveyed her closely—aquamarine sundress and a designer scarf, not-too-deep crow's-feet, pouting lips, high, possibly padded bustline, delicate hands. He figured her for around his age, late thirties. It was her general demeanor, perhaps, that reminded him of Monica. Monica...hell, he couldn't keep his mind off her for a moment. And he had tried. For eighteen miserable months she had been the focus of his thoughts.

The woman counted change into his hand. He thanked her, shoved the money into a trouser pocket. "Did anyone ever tell you you look like a policeman?" she said.

Eddie Sands grinned as if proud, ran his hand across his trim ivy-league-cut hair. "I guess it's the short hair that gives me away," he said.

"I noticed the handcuffs when you took out your wallet," she said. "Are you with the city?"

Sands shook his head. "No, ma'am, I'm a lieutenant with the Las Vegas Police Department," he said.

The woman gave him another icy smile, said she loved Vegas, then turned to help another customer.

At the pay phone outside, he dialed a Beverly Hills number. Bruce O'Hara, whose voice was unmistakable, answered. Without saying anything, Sands set the receiver back on the hook. He returned to the sedan, climbed in, then started the engine and pulled into traffic. He checked his wristwatch: three o'clock. He wound out of the crowded business area, crossed Santa Monica Boulevard, and headed into a palm-lined residential area where wide, well-washed thoroughfares were lined with palatial Mission, Victorian, and Colonial revivals. As he drove, he checked a Beverly Hills city map he'd picked up earlier at a service station. Two more turns and he found himself in front of an imposing two-story Mission-style home on Rexford Drive. He turned directly into the circular driveway.

He climbed out of the sedan, walked across a small fuchsia-lined courtyard which protected the front door. He took a deep breath, then pressed the doorbell. The sound of footsteps came from inside. The peephole opened. Sands held up a badge. "Las Vegas Police Department. I'd like to speak with Mr. Bruce O'Hara."

The door opened. Bruce O'Hara, who looked shorter, grayer, and more wrinkled than he did on the screen or in movie-magazine photographs, was wearing Levi's, loafers, and a chamois-cloth shirt. A sixty-year-old millionaire movie idol trying to look like the thirty-year-old guy next door.

"*Las Vegas* Police Department?" O'Hara said as he glanced at the Nevada license plate on the sedan. "What's this all about?"

"It's a confidential matter," Sands said. "I'd like to speak with you about something that occurred when you were in Las Vegas."

O'Hara looked about suspiciously. "May I see your police identification card?"

"Certainly." Sands dug into his inside jacket pocket. He handed O'Hara a laminated identification card.

O'Hara examined the card, handed it back. "A confidential matter, says the detective. Sounds like an opening scene from one of my movies."

Sands gave a polite laugh as O'Hara ushered him inside and led him down a short hallway into an enormous living room decorated with wall hangings, pillows, and blankets in a red-black-and-brown pattern that Sands guessed would be called Navajo. The sofa, chairs, and walls were earth-colored, and there was a roughly hewn wooden candelabra next to a gold-tone telephone on a coffee table. A celluloid cowboy's house.

O'Hara motioned Sands to a sofa. From a hand-carved wooden box he removed a cigarette.

"I'm a dectective lieutenant, Mr. O'Hara," Sands said as he sat down. "I'm in charge of homicide investigations."

O'Hara raised his hands in a gesture of surrender. "I

didn't do it, officer," he said histrionically.

Sands gave him a professional courtesy smile. From his shirt pocket he removed a photograph of an attractive, thirtyish platinum blonde. He shoved the photograph across the coffee table. "Recognize her?"

O'Hara examined the photograph. "Never seen her before in my life." He tossed the photo back to Sands, lit the cigarette, took a big pull. Then he sat back and crossed his legs. The loafers were Ballys.

Sands shoved the photograph back into his pocket. "She says she knows you."

"What the hell is this all about?" O'Hara said. "This interview is ended unless you tell me what this is all about."

Sands leaned forward, he folded his hands. "A week ago that woman's husband was sleeping in his apartment in Las Vegas and someone shot him six times with a .32. There were no signs of forced entry into the apartment, so whoever killed him had to have access. In other words, it was someone he knew."

"Just what does this have to do with me?"

"I'm not finished."

"Excuse me."

"Our investigation determined that the woman owned a .32 revolver and that she'd been having violent arguments with her husband. Once she threatened to kill him. When we questioned her, she maintained her innocence. So we gave her a lie-detector test. Unfortunately, the test was inconclusive. The polygraph operator couldn't tell whether she was lying or telling the truth. That's why I'm here."

Maintaining eye contact, Sands paused a moment before continuing. "The woman gave us a statement claiming she was with you on the night of the murder."

O'Hara uncrossed, then crossed his legs again. "Mental hospitals are full of people who say they've been with a movie star at this time or that," he said.

Sands took a piece of paper from his jacket pocket and unfolded it. He read aloud:

"'I, Helen Stinson Calabrese, having been warned of

my constitutional right to remain silent, and without duress of any kind, wish to make the following statement voluntarily and of my own free will. I am a prostitute and work out of the bar in the Stardust Hotel on Las Vegas Boulevard. On August seventeenth I received word from a bellman who acts as my pimp that I had a customer waiting in the penthouse suite of the hotel. I went to the suite and the man who opened the door was a guy with a goatee whom I recognized as a previous customer. I think he is a movie producer or a movie lawyer or something like that. Or at least that is what he told me last month when I first met him. He told me that he had a friend in the next room who had some special requests. We talked it over and settled on the price of six hundred dollars. Then he gave me a room key and I went to the penthouse suite and met Mr. Bruce O'Hara, the movie star. I know it was him because I have seen almost all of his movies. I stayed the night with Mr. O'Hara. I remember this night in particular not only because Mr. O'Hara is a movie star, but because of his special requests. He asked me to dress in a black rubber suit, which he provided, and to use hat pins to—'"

"I think at this point it might be better if you directed any questions you have to my lawyer, Mickey Greene," O'Hara interrupted. He stubbed his cigarette into the ashtray, came to his feet, folded his arms across his chest. "He's an expert at libel cases—movie-magazine lies."

"I'd like to explain something," Sands said. The thought occurred to him that the comedians who did impressions of O'Hara invariably mimicked the way he folded his arms. "This woman is in jail facing the charge of murder. If she *is* lying, if she's concocted an alibi, that's one thing. On the other hand, if she *is* telling the truth, it means she's innocent and should be released."

Bruce O'Hara's usually expressive mouth was a fine line. He stared at his Navajo blanket drapes as if he'd never seen them before.

Speaking slowly and clearly, Sands continued. "There

are, at this moment, only four people who are aware of this woman's alibi—you and me, my captain, and the woman's lawyer. There has been no publicity. Also, you should be aware that the victim was a small-time drug dealer who had lots of enemies and no friends. I guess what I am trying to say is that the problem is still...uh ...*manageable*. It can be handled discreetly, if you know what I mean."

O'Hara snatched the phone receiver off the cradle. "I'm going to phone my attorney," he said.

"Once you bring in the attorney, our options are limited," Sands said as O'Hara dialed. "What I'm telling you is that for a few bucks the problem can be washed."

O'Hara stopped dialing. Slowly, he set the receiver down. Cautiously, and without looking Sands in the eye, he lifted the cover of the cigarette box, picked up a smoke, hung it on his lip. "Care for a drink?"

"You bet."

Sands followed the movie star through a wide doorway into an expansive wood-paneled den. The walls were decorated with everything from a ship's angel to carved wooden duck decoys. On the mantel above the fireplace stood oriental vases. O'Hara stepped behind a bar that must have been twelve feet long and asked Sands what he'd like to drink. Sands said scotch. O'Hara set two glasses on the bar and filled them three fingers high.

"I don't know if you're aware of this," Sands said. "But cops look up to you. Your movies show cops in a good light. And on the talk shows you always have good things to say about law-enforcement people. You're not one of those left-wing movie types."

O'Hara forced a smile as he dropped ice in the drinks.

"I guess what I'm saying is that no self-respecting cop, including myself, would want to see your career ruined by a lot of bad publicity."

"This...uh...prostitute. You say she is represented by an attorney?"

Sands picked up his drink. "Who happens to be an old

14

friend of mine." He sipped and swallowed. "Las Vegas is a very small town, in certain ways."

"I see." O'Hara downed half his drink and set the glass back on the bar.

Sands cleared his throat. "At this point I'm in control of the situation. No one has talked to the press."

"I'm more than willing to handle the matter...uh... discreetly, but I'd prefer to have my attorney here to represent me. Is that too much to ask?"

"There are too many people involved as it is," Sands said. "And the time bomb is ticking."

O'Hara had a perplexed look, an expression like nothing Sands had ever seen him use on screen. "If you choose to bring your lawyer in, everything is on the record from here on out," Sands said. "You will have lost the opportunity to handle things painlessly."

O'Hara downed the rest of his drink, stared into the glass. "What is it going to take?"

"Money."

"How *much* money?"

"Fifty thousand dollars."

"Out of the question."

"Twenty thousand goes to my captain. The lawyer and the prostitute will settle for fifteen. I get fifteen. That's a total of fifty."

"So, you have it all figured out."

"Yes, sir."

O'Hara stabbed an index finger at Sands's face. *"Look,* fella," he hissed. "Right now you have as much to lose as I do. I have violated no law. *You* are the one who just solicited a bribe. That's *extortion.* I could pick up the phone and turn you in right at this very moment. I could call your chief...or the governor of the State of Nevada!"

Calmly, Sands examined his palms. He curled his fingers, checked his nails. "If you do, my captain will back up the story that I came here to interview you and you attempted to bribe me. There would be an internal-affairs investigation by the department, but it would be your word against mine. Your complaint would be ruled unfounded. In the meantime, the whore's statement would be leaked to the press. In the end the worst thing that would happen to me is that I might be transferred out of the Detective Bureau. You, on the other hand, will have had your linen washed in the *National Enquirer*. Comedians will make jokes about you. Your career will be fucked."

O'Hara picked up a pack of cigarettes off the bar, lit up, blew a sharp stream of smoke.

"I agree," he said finally, "that the best way to handle the...uh...matter is as you've suggested. But I'd like to think about it. If you'll leave a card I'll get back to you."

"That's not the way it works," Sands said. "Either I leave here with the money or nature takes its course."

O'Hara fondled the bridge of his nose for a moment. Suddenly, he turned and reached for a wall-mounted phone behind the bar. "I need to speak with my attorney," he said as he lifted the receiver.

Sands climbed off the bar stool as O'Hara dialed. "Thanks for the drink," he said. On his way across the living room, he thought his heart would pound out of his chest. Hesitantly, he reached for the door handle. *Should he say anything else or just get the hell out?*

"Please wait just a moment," O'Hara said.

Sands's eyes closed, then opened. He turned around.

Bruce O'Hara was standing at the entrance to the den. "I'll pay," he said.

2 On the way to the bank, Bruce O'Hara sat in the passenger seat of the sedan. He wore a golf hat and dark glasses, which he said he always wore to keep from being recognized in public. Sands carefully maintained the speed limit along crowded Wilshire Boulevard. "Do you know the bank manager?" Sands said.

"Fairly well."

"Keep it light. Tell him the money is to pay off a poker debt. Ask him to be discreet. It's the first time you've gambled in years and you're embarrassed."

O'Hara pointed to a multistory smoked-glass building on the right. "That's it." Sands pulled to the curb in front. O'Hara climbed out, walked toward the front door. As he entered, Sands put the car in gear and made a U-turn. He pulled to the curb across the street, a location which provided an unobstructed view of the front of the bank in case O'Hara called the police from inside.

Though his eyes remained riveted on the bank, he still couldn't get Monica off his mind. He clearly imagined swimming naked with her in a heated Las Vegas pool, cupping her breasts, tasting her full, wet lips.

He checked his wristwatch. It had been five minutes.

Finally, Bruce O'Hara stepped out of the bank. He was carrying a briefcase. He looked about. Sands shoved his hand out the passenger window and waved. O'Hara looked both ways, stepped off the curb.

"Bring me your money, motherfucker," Sands said out loud to himself as the movie star jogged across Wilshire Boulevard toward him. He started the engine.

"I have a question," O'Hara said as he climbed into the passenger seat. Sands pulled into traffic.

"Yes, sir," Sands said as if replying to a superior officer.

"If I hand this money to you right now, what's to stop you from coming back tomorrow and asking for another fifty thousand?"

"Once I take the money, I have violated the law," Sands said as he made a left turn on Beverly Drive. "I won't chance coming back, because I might walk into a police trap. Besides, I'm not greedy."

"What if you spread this money around and it doesn't do any good? What if the woman refuses to keep her mouth shut?"

"The moment you hand me the money I assume full and total responsibility for fixing the entire problem. If the woman squawks, I, one way or the other, will stop her from squawking."

O'Hara sat back in the seat as Sands turned onto Rexford Drive. "You're experienced at this sort of thing, aren't you?" Without a reply, Sands slowed down. He steered the sedan into the driveway of O'Hara's residence and pulled up to the house.

"I never thought anything like this would happen to me," O'Hara said in a mournful tone.

In order to push things along, Sands made a show of checking his wristwatch.

"I feel like telling you to go straight to hell," O'Hara said as he dropped the briefcase on the seat and climbed out of the car. Without looking back, he walked briskly toward his mansion.

As Sands drove out of sight of O'Hara's house, he used one hand to open the briefcase. He reached in, pulled out a stack of banded hundred-dollar bills, thumbed it. Then he let out his breath.

Just outside the Beverly Hills city limit, Sands stopped at a pay telephone across the street from a health-food restaurant and dialed a Las Vegas number which he knew by heart.

"Pan American Investors," Monica said.

"It's me, baby."

"What happened?" she said nervously.

"It's down."

"How much did he go for?"

"Fifty."

"I was so worried, honey. I love you."

"Will Parisi front the money?"

"He says that's no problem. He'll turn the key."

"I'm gonna be on you soon, babe. I'm gonna be on you like a dog."

"You're all I think about, Eddie. I love you so much. I want you in me right now. I wish you were here right now to fuck me and suck my tits."

Eddie Sands checked his wristwatch. It was almost four-thirty. "I've got a time factor, hon. I love you more than ever."

As Monica made kisses into the phone he set the receiver back on the hook.

He hurried back to the car and sped out of the parking space, heading straight for the Harbor Freeway. Arriving in San Pedro, he steered across the Vincent Thomas Bridge to Terminal Island. On Ferry Street he parked the sedan behind a rusting cargo container sitting in an abandoned marine-salvage yard. With the engine running, he removed his gun, handcuffs, and bullet pouch, then used a screwdriver to remove the Nevada license plates from the sedan and install California plates. He placed all the items along with the briefcase in the trunk of the vehicle, then closed and locked it.

He checked his wristwatch, noted that it was ten minutes before five, and broke into a jog down Ferry Street. He ran past a deserted tuna cannery, breathing hard. As he approached the black rocks at the water's edge, he veered left past a large green metal sign which read "Terminal Island Federal Penitentiary." He crossed the prison parking lot and went up the steps of the prison's administration building, a brownstone structure which, without its high fences and gun towers, could easily have been mistaken for some prewar educational institution.

Entering through the main door, Sands stepped into a reception area where a muscle-bound black guard sat behind a bulletproof glass partition reading a paperback book titled *Ripley's Believe It or Not.* As he approached, the guard looked up at him, pressed a lever. Slowly, a door of bars to the right of the guard station began to roll into the wall.

Sands entered, moved down a short hallway to a door above which was a stenciled sign. It read "Work Release Program—Inmates Only." He entered a musty-smelling, crowded room. He stripped off his civilian clothing and arranged it on a hanger. After placing the hanger on a long rack fashioned from half-inch pipe, he took a place at the end of a line of naked prisoners.

As he reached the front of the line, a flashlight-toting guard, known because of his height, girth, and general demeanor as the Little King, barked his usual: "Hands on top of your head, hands down, shake your hands through your hair, turn around, bend over, spread your cheeks."

The Little King's flashlight clicked on, then off. Sands stood up, and, as a prisoner behind him submitted to the same humiliation, he moved into the next room and donned his baggy denim prison clothes. He used a government ballpoint pen to fill out a preprinted form titled "Inmate Work Release Activity Report." Completed, it read as follows:

Where did you report for work today?
Mel's Used Cars and Rental Service
1400 South Central Avenue
Los Angeles
What kind of work did you perform?
Used-car salesman
What hours did you work?
7:30 a.m.—4:00 p.m.

With the knowledge that the ex-con manager at the used-car lot would cover for him if questioned, he tossed the completed form into a brimming wire basket on the corner of the table.

Then he headed back to his one-man cell.

There Eddie Sands reached for a transistor radio on the shelf above his bunk. He adjusted the dial to the Dr. Paul Lofgren show. Lofgren, a mellow-voiced talk-show psychologist, calmly asked a woman caller when she had first had sex. Without a hint of embarrassment in her voice the woman said it had happened when she was seventeen years old in the backseat of a car. Holding the radio to his ear, Eddie Sands leaned against the bars as Dr. Lofgren and the woman continued to talk. He closed his eyes and imagined himself in the backseat of his car with his high school girlfriend, whom he had not thought of in many years. He removed her blouse, then her brassiere. Young, hard-bodied, she lifted one leg at a time as he pulled off her panties. She was wet and he could smell her. Now she was Monica.

Dr. Paul Lofgren signed off the air, and there was a blast of rock music. Immediately, Sands turned off the radio, set it back on the shelf. He rolled up his sleeves and washed at the sink. Using a clean towel, he dried his hands and face thoroughly and lay down on his bunk. Lying there, with the indentations in the two-inch mattress he'd been sleeping on for eighteen months fitting his back perfectly, he concentrated on familiar sounds—the murmur of television sets and radios echoing along the cell block, muffled conversations, the ever-present thumping of metal pipes which seemed to emanate from the prison cement like a mysterious heartbeat. He closed his eyes and imagined a naked Monica straddling him, lowering her breasts to his face, whispering to him.

Then a familiar buzzer sounded three short bursts. It was dinnertime.

3

The prison dining hall, a high-ceil-inged room filled with round Formica-covered tables, was crowded. The walls were covered with crude in-mate-art murals which depicted mus-cular black and brown men pulling ropes and lifting beams. As Eddie Sands moved along the busy chow line, black and brown men who looked much less athletic than the figures in the murals used slotted serving spoons to fill the indentations on his plastic tray with the stock items he had vowed to never eat again once he was re-leased: tasteless macaroni, white bread, canned peaches, soggy broccoli.

Carrying a brimming tray, he moved to his usual table in the voluntarily segregated white area of the hall. Having taken his seat at the empty table, he picked at his meal.

A few minutes later, Pepper Lopez, a wiry Mexican with long, slicked-back hair and crooked teeth, came to the table. He set his tray across from Sands and sat down.

"Tell them I'm through with work release," Sands said. "They can sell it to someone else. I'm not long for this place."

The Mexican chuckled, showing his teeth, as he pushed food here and there on his tray. "What are you talking about, man?"

"I'm getting out on an appeal."

"What kind of an appeal?" Lopez said as he folded a slice of white bread and took a large bite out of the middle.

"What's the difference?"

"I'm getting out in two days myself, man," Lopez said. "Maybe I'll look you up."

"Feel free," Sands said, though both he and the other man knew they would probably never see each other again.

The modern Las Vegas Federal Courthouse, situated within view of the downtown casinos, was less than crowded.

John Novak, a clean-featured man who moved with the confident gait of a soldier (hell, fifteen years in the FBI wasn't that much different than fifteen in the army), made his way down a marbled hallway past courtroom doors. Though he felt at home in such public places, as well as in all types of underworld nests, he was no longer affected very much by either. He had come to know the shared secret of all veteran cops—that the face of crime wouldn't be changed one iota by his efforts.

His general appearance was not distinguished by any noticeable trait. Though he wore wing-tip shoes, a bland necktie, a suit purchased in a discount clothing store—attire that in a courtroom crowd would have rendered him invisible—a trained observer would never mistake him for a lawyer, court clerk, or defendant. It was the mournful, piercing quality of his eyes. Like the eyes of most cops, they reflected world-weariness and a heart hardened to the fact that the endless platoons of criminals and victims, defense lawyers and prosecutors, cops and special agents, parole and probation officers, judges and jailers, would continue to march long after he was dead and gone.

He had brown hair, which was graying prematurely, and the solid build of a wrestler. He was proud that as a student at Pennsylvania State University he had wrestled his way to the national collegiate wrestling championship in the 165-pound class.

He was no longer disappointed that the nights he had worked without overtime pay, that the stress which had caused his divorce (a marriage counselor told him he hadn't been home long enough to notice the deterioration of his marriage), that the sixty-three days he had spent in the Queen of Angels Hospital recovering from a punctured lung after a knife attack by prison escapee Durward Elroy Huggins, who later escaped again, that all those sacrifices and the indiscriminate transfers to various posts of duty which circumscribed him at age forty-one to being an apartment-dweller with nothing more to his name than a .30-30 deer rifle, some utilitarian furniture, and a gold wristwatch given to him as a birthday gift by Judge Lorraine Traynor, were meaningless in the big picture.

But even with this dark, though in his mind quite realistic, view, he still held the hope that the hoods he went after would at least have had their asses puckered knowing that John Novak, a Philadelphia policeman's son who had been the first in his family to graduate college, had worked on the case.

He reached a door at the end of the hall marked "Lorraine Traynor—U.S. District Judge." He carefully opened the courtroom door a few inches, peeked in. The judge, an attractive woman of his age with striking blue eyes, looked down from the bench and made eye contact with him. She gave a subtle nod. Quietly, he closed the courtroom door and made his way to the parking lot outside.

A few minutes later, as Novak sat in his government sedan smoking a cigarette, Lorraine Traynor, having changed from her judicial robe into a dark skirt and sweater, made her way down the courthouse steps and headed toward the sedan. She climbed in the passenger door and, having glanced about to make sure no one was looking, kissed him on the cheek.

"So where have you been for the past week?" she said as he started the engine.

"Working on the Parisi case."

"The Parisi case. Everyone is working on the Parisi case."

"Did you miss me?" he said with a wry grin.

"Not at all."

Novak steered onto Fremont Boulevard and drove past a block filled with garishly decorated marriage chapels, pawnshops, and fast-food restaurants.

"The senior judge called me in yesterday. He told me that the other judges frowned on the fact that I was dating an FBI agent."

"What did you say?"

"I told him my personal life was none of his business," she said. "When do you get paid?"

"Day after tomorrow."

"Then you probably don't have enough money to take me to dinner tonight?"

"Right."

At Novak's modestly furnished apartment they headed straight into the bedroom. Lorraine Traynor moved past an unmade bed to a dressing table. She unfastened the pearl necklace she was wearing and set it next to a framed photograph of Novak with his father and brother in their police uniforms. "I learned something about you the other day," she said.

"Whatsat?" Novak said as he unfastened his necktie and tossed it onto a chair.

"Someone told me you were transferred from the FBI

office to the Organized Crime Strike Force because you were having simultaneous affairs with two female agents." She unzipped her skirt. It dropped to the floor. She stepped out of it.

Novak's shirt, trousers, and underwear piled up in the chair.

Lorraine Traynor lifted the sweater over her head. She wore no bra. "Did you hear what I said?"

Novak moved to her. From behind, he cupped her breasts.

"Why won't you answer me?" she said.

"Shut up," he whispered softly as his hands slid down between her legs. She turned to him. As they kissed, Novak felt her nails dig into his back.

On the bed they screwed fiercely, and a perspiring U.S. District Judge Lorraine Traynor, her legs raised in the victory sign, gave little pleasure yelps as the bed rocked and they inched closer to orgasm.

After lovemaking, she hugged him tightly.

"I want you to help me write an affidavit for a bug," he whispered.

"Who's the target?"

"Tony Parisi."

"I thought you told me he uses different phones?"

"That's why I want your help."

They climbed out of bed, took separate showers, and dressed.

In his small but relatively neat kitchen, he made drinks as she unwrapped a small beef roast and popped it into the microwave oven.

"Who else are you seeing?" she said on her way to the sink. She turned on a faucet.

He handed her a drink. "No one."

"I don't care. But I want you to tell me."

"Why?"

"What's the big difficulty in making a case on Parisi?" she said in order to change the subject.

"Parisi seems to know what we're going to do before we do it. It's as if he has an instinct."

After dinner, Novak cleaned off the kitchen table and

for the next hour or so recited facts about Parisi's criminal activities to Lorraine as she scribbled the draft of an electronic eavesdropping affidavit. Finally, the affidavit was finished. Completed, it read as follows:

The following affidavit is in support of a request for a court order to use electronic means to eavesdrop on one Anthony Salvatore Parisi.

I, John Novak, hereby depose and say:
I am a Special Agent of the Federal Bureau of Investigation presently assigned to the Department of Justice Strike Force Against Organized Crime and Racketeering. I have been so employed for more than fifteen years, specializing in organized-crime cases while assigned to the New York, Chicago, and Los Angeles field offices. Due to my experience and training I have been qualified in various federal courts as an expert on organized crime, and specifically, the criminal syndicate known commonly as La Cosa Nostra or the Mafia.

For the past eighteen months I have been assigned to an investigation of one Anthony Salvatore Parisi, aka Tough Tony, whom I know to be a ranking member of the Vacarillo La Cosa Nostra crime family.

Approximately fifteen months ago, numerous reports were received by the FBI from persons holding management positions in various Las Vegas casinos that they had been victims of extortion perpetrated by representatives of the Vacarillo crime family. Many of the extortion threats were made by associates of Anthony Parisi who are known to me. Many of the threats were made by one Vito Fanducci (FBI #929486133), whom I know to be an employee of Parisi and who has, in the past, acted as a "muscle" and collector for him. Both Parisi and Fanducci are convicted felons who have served sentences for both Interstate Travel in Aid of Racketeering and Second Degree Murder.

Following these initial extortion reports, there in fact were three murders (see the attached police reports) of casino employees who held supervisory positions in Las Vegas casinos. Two of the victims were casino count-room managers and one was a pit boss. Subsequent investigation determined that all three decedents had refused to go along with extortionate demands made by Parisi through his underlings. Also, physical evidence gathered during the investigation of the murders showed that all three victims were murdered in the same manner: gunshots to the head as they were either coming from or going to the casinos where they were employed. After this, confidential sources in Las Vegas casinos reported to me that the three casinos involved began secretly paying extortion money to Parisi on a regular basis.

Since that time, I have used every standard investigatory technique in an attempt to gather evidence of Parisi's involvement in this continuing criminal enterprise, namely extortion involving Las Vegas casinos, but to no avail. Parisi operates out of rooms authorized for his use by various hotel/casino managers who fear recrimination if they contact the authorities and uses house phones to conduct his illegal business in order to avoid having his discussions of criminal dealings detected by means of a court-authorized wiretap. During this time, all extortion victims or other witnesses whom I have interviewed have refused to testify against Parisi in open court because they fear for their lives.

It is therefore my belief that the installation of listening devices, including a wiretap on the telephone instrument in whatever room Parisi is currently using at the Stardust Hotel, would assist in the gathering of evidence of violations of the fed-

eral law being committed by Parisi and his co-
horts.

They moved into the living room, and like some
dumpy married couple, as Lorraine put it, they lounged
about and watched television—a B mystery movie
which Novak figured was better than anything else that
was on.

"Do you actually enjoy your work?" she said as she
leaned her head on his shoulder.

"How do you mean?"

"I mean, if you finished law school you could be a
lawyer."

Novak shook his head. "The whole judicial system
makes me sick."

"But you are part of the judicial system."

"Wrong. The judicial system lets crooks *out* of jail. I
put them *in* jail."

"So as a judge, I guess I'm the person who decides
whether someone is or is not a crook."

"Wrong. You're someone who lets the crooks out of
jail."

"I also send crooks *to* jail."

"Do you think Parisi is a crook?"

"Everyone knows he's a crook. He's probably the biggest crook in Las Vegas."

"Then why don't you put him in jail?" Novak said.

"Because it's not part of my job."

"But on the other hand, if I arrested him and failed to
follow correct procedure you would let him *out* of jail,
right?"

"That's our system."

"See what I mean?"

Though it was something she seldom did, Lorraine
Traynor stayed the night.

4 Early the next morning, Novak drove Lorraine Traynor to the federal courthouse. She said, "Don't be such a stranger," as she gathered up her briefcase and purse. She touched her lips briefly to his cheek, climbed out of the car. Novak checked his wristwatch, pulled into traffic. He believed in arriving early to meetings with informants.

And Novak knew informants were the name of the game. They were the lifeblood of every prosecution, and thus a constant source of strife and bitterness among the FBI, the Federal Bureau of Narcotics, the U.S. Treasury's Bureau of Alcohol, Tobacco and Firearms, the investigative arms of the Internal Revenue Service and the Department of Labor—all the competing agencies that staffed the Organized Crime Strike Force.

Novak remembered that the Strike Force was originally founded in order to stop the bickering over federal informants. The plan was that each agency would assign one above-average, highly motivated special agent to work under seasoned government prosecutors. Thus cooperation among the agencies would force a united front against the sophisticated leaders of organized crime.

But in government work, as Novak had learned over the years, all such task forces eventually deteriorated into competing duchies of bureaucratic self-interest.

Therefore, rather than stopping the competition for informants, as was intended, the Strike Force institutionalized it. Rather than above-average, highly motivated special agents and seasoned prosecutors, the various law-enforcement agencies assigned agents who were either problem children, drones, or retired-on-the-job types. The prosecutor slots were filled with either young lawyers who'd worked on the last presidential campaign, oddball assistant U.S. attorneys who couldn't find any other way to get transferred out of Washington, D.C., or glory seekers who realized that the easiest way to get reporters to attend a press conference at the federal courthouse was to mention the words "organized crime."

A half hour or so later, John Novak was sitting in a window booth of the Highland Coffee Shop, a modern-looking place located a mile or so off the Las Vegas Strip. Having finished breakfast, he kept his eyes on the entrance to the parking lot. As he sat there among tables filled with people reading glossy menus and eating mediocre food, he mused about how much time he'd spent in similar establishments during the last fifteen years— time spent not because he enjoyed greasy fare or the lingering smell of cigarette smoke, but because, whether it was in Newark, New Orleans, Miami, L.A., or Las Vegas, it was just plain safer to meet informants in public places.

Bruno Santoro's black Cadillac cruised by the front of the restaurant and into the parking lot. Novak checked his wristwatch. Bruno was on time.

Quickly, Novak left the table and moved to the cashier. He took bills from a well-worn leather case which also held his badge and identification card and paid up.

Outside, as Bruno parked his Cadillac, Novak stood near the entrance for a moment. He surveyed the lot carefully. Still trying to think of a new tack to use on Bruno, he moved across the parking lot to his government sedan, which was parked at the other end of the lot facing Bruno's car. He unlocked the driver's door, climbed in behind the wheel. Having given the lot another once-over, he pulled the headlight switch of the G-car: on and off twice. Immediately the headlights of Bruno's Cadillac returned the same signal.

The Cadillac pulled up next to Novak's car. The diminutive Bruno, wearing a rumpled sharkskin suit and eyeglasses with sleek frames matching his gray hair, exited the Cadillac and moved to the passenger side of Novak's car. He glanced about, straightened his silk tie unnecessarily, opened the passenger door, and climbed in. Immediately, he pulled a fresh package of Camels out of his jacket pocket.

"Parisi's been acting funny all week," Bruno said as he tore cellophane from the cigarette package. "And yesterday there was a car parked down the street from my apartment with two guys sitting in it. For all I know, Tony has paper out on me right this very minute. I might be a dead man already." He tapped a cigarette out of the pack, hung it on his lip.

"Maybe it's just your imagination."

Bruno flamed the cigarette with a gold lighter. He turned his head slightly and emptied his lungs of smoke. "Look, G-man," he said finally, "I don't have no imagination. I grew up in a reform school. I been with rounders the whole fuckin' fifty-three years of my life. I'm telling you the man is treating me differently."

"Differently like how?"

"He doesn't really *tell* me anything anymore. That's why all I've been able to get for you in the last couple of weeks is bits and pieces."

"So bits and pieces are better than nothing," Novak said.

"So waking up in the morning is better than sleeping with the fishes."

"What have you heard this week?" Novak said.

"Like I said . . . bits and pieces. Something about Tony paying off somebody on the Federal Prison Board."

"You mean the Federal Parole Board," Novak said.

"Whoever does the springing of people from federal joints."

"Who does Tony want sprung?"

"It's somebody who's gonna work for him, or do something for him, make some money for him. Some shit like that. I don't have a name." Bruno puffed more smoke. He coughed softly.

"Anything else?" Novak said.

"Bruce O'Hara."

"I take it you mean the movie actor?"

Bruno gave an impatient nod. "After my shift at the blackjack table I'm sitting at the bar in the Stardust. Tony gets a call. I hear him say the guy's name."

"That's all? He just mentioned his name?"

Bruno nodded. "I want off the fucking hook," he said after a pause. "Things are too hot for me and I want out."

Expressionless, Novak folded his hands. "I thought we had a deal."

"When we made our deal you promised me I could pull out if things started getting hot. You said I could pull out anytime I wanted."

"I need you in there with him. You're my only source of information."

"You told me that when the time came you would move me. You promised to set me up with a new identity."

Novak nodded slowly as he tried to think of a way to change the subject.

Bruno tapped ashes into the dashboard tray. "I kept my part of the bargain. I've been a rat against Tony. I helped you lock up three people who work for him. Now I want a moving van and a new name."

"The deal was that if I fixed things with the Strike Force attorneys and convinced the judge to let you stay on the street, you would do Tony for me."

Bruno rubbed his eyes, ran fingers through his hair. "I've tried. I've done every fuckin' thing I can think of to help you make a case on him. You know that."

"I can't ask the judge to suspend your sentence because you were *trying* to put Tony in the joint. She'll laugh at me. You know how federal judges are."

Bruno stared out the window. "I know how you feds are too," he said finally. "You like to squeeze people for everything you can get."

"If you suddenly just drop out of sight, Tony'll know it was you."

"By then I'll be in the wind."

"I think you're worried about nothing," Novak said. "If Tony had put out a contract on you, I would have heard about it from another source already. These things get around."

"So if you got so many rats on the street, why do you need me?"

Novak massaged the steering wheel. "All I'm asking is that you keep your ears open for one more week. Then, if you still want out, I'll take you into the witness protection program. That's a promise."

Bruno looked at his cigarette. "That's the same double-talk you gave me last week."

Because it was, Novak said nothing.

"I shoulda known you people would end up fucking me in the ass," he said. "If I had it to do over I would just go do my time instead of putting all my friends in jail."

"All I'm asking is one more week."

Bruno opened the wind wing and pushed the cigarette out. He fidgeted. "You'd do anything to get Tony. You could care less what happens to me." Rapidly, he lit another smoke.

Novak bit his lip for a moment. "You refused to testify about Tony before the federal grand jury. So the attorney-in-charge of the Organized Crime Strike Force won't approve witness protection."

"Fuck the attorney-in-charge," Bruno said angrily. "You gave me *your* word. That's why I went along with what you wanted me to do. I believed *you*."

"All I'm asking is a few more days."

For a moment, Bruno Santoro examined his well-manicured dealer's nails. Then he reached for the door handle.

"It'll look better for the judge if you testify against Tony in front of the federal grand jury," Novak said. "It'll help your case."

Bruno shook his head in dismay. He took two deep puffs on his cigarette. "It's always just one more thing," he said sadly. "Every time we meet you squeeze me for one more thing."

"You can testify in secret."

"Tony has ways of finding out shit like that," Bruno said after a while.

"But like you said, by then you'll be in the wind."

Bruno took a deep drag from his cigarette. He rolled the window down and flicked it a long way. "Are you telling me that if I testify I won't have to go to the joint?"

"I can't make you any promises—"

"Is that what you're telling me?" Bruno interrupted.

Novak nodded.

Bruno swallowed and cleared his throat.

"When I was twenty years old this family guy who was running broads calls me into his restaurant. He tells me a guy named Guido fucked him out of some money and went to Florida. The family guy asks me if I want the contract. I'm hungry. Guido is an asshole. So I take the paper. I find Guido in Florida, case the place where he was staying. He was with his kids." Mournfully, Bruno shook his head, stared into the distance.

"What happened?" Novak said.

"That night I checked into a motel and I tried to get my balls up—to talk myself into doing it, you know? The family guy keeps calling me. I kept putting him off, picking up the gun, putting it down. But I just couldn't do it. Even though I knew I wouldn't be able to show my face in the neighborhood ever again, I still fucking couldn't kill anyone." He turned to face Novak. "If I woulda been smart, instead of coming to Vegas I woulda joined the navy or something. My father wanted me to join the navy. Fuck."

"The grand jury meets tomorrow," Novak said. "I'll pick you up here."

Bruno sat there a moment. "It's the last thing I'm doing for you people," he said.

Then he opened the passenger door and climbed out.

5 Red Haynes, a lanky, sleepy-eyed man with fiery tousled hair and over-sized ears, sat in the stuffy waiting room of the Federal Health Clinic. His arms were folded across his chest. Seated opposite him was an emaciated, stringy-haired woman wearing an extremely short skirt. He watched as, keeping her knees primly together, the woman nervously reapplied both lipstick and pancake makeup for the third time during the twenty minutes or so that he had been waiting. A wired-up pillhead, he said to himself.

To Haynes's right was a fortyish man dressed in a bu-reaucrat's uniform—short-sleeved white shirt with ball-point-pen marks on the pocket, baggy trousers, and cheap wing-tipped shoes. Come to think of it, Haynes said to himself, except for the on-sale polyester sport coat that covered his gun and handcuffs, he was dressed the same way.

A door opened. A tall, bubble-butted black nurse stepped into the room. "Agent Haynes?"

"That's me."

"Dr. Rhodes will see you now."

Red Haynes came to his feet and shuffled behind bubble-butt into the doctor's office. The doctor, a parrot-nosed man much younger than Haynes, looked up from his paperwork and nodded. Haynes took a seat in front of the desk. On the walls were diplomas, psychiatric-internship certificates, other crapola which impressed Haynes about as much as a television commercial. The door closed behind him.

"Your file says you've been an FBI agent for twenty years," the doctor said as he removed his thick glasses and wiped the lenses, then the frames, on a small rag.

"Right."

"Do you know why you're here?"

"Because I received a low yearly performance evaluation and the agent-in-charge said I'm depressed."

"Do you think you're depressed?"

"No."

Dr. Rhodes nodded his parrot beak. "Why do you suppose your supervisor said you were depressed?"

"To screw me."

"Why do you think your supervisor would want to... uh...to cause you problems?"

Red Haynes interlaced his bony fingers. With a brisk, well-practiced movement, he loudly cracked his knuckles. The doctor winced.

"Because that's the way he is."

"What do you mean by that?"

"He is an asshole."

"And you feel he wants to cause you harm?"

Haynes shook his head. "If you are born an asshole you cause people harm whether you want to or not."

Dr. Rhodes lifted his eyeglasses from his nose for an unnecessary cleaning, lenses only this time, then tipped them back onto the deep eyeglass indentation on his beak. "Do you ever have nightmares?"

"I did a few years ago."

"What were they about?"

"Shooting somebody."

"Anyone in particular?"

"A bank robber."

"What was occurring in your life around the time you started having those nightmares?"

"I'd just shot a bank robber with a twelve-gauge shotgun."

Dr. Rhodes stared at Haynes for a moment, as if doing so would help solve some great riddle. "What did you do immediately after the shooting?"

"I went to a bar with the other agents. We celebrated."

"And it was after that you began to have nightmares?"

"That very night."

"What occurred during the nightmares?"

"I would shoot the guy and see the blood and gore all over again. It was in Technicolor."

"Perhaps you felt guilty about what had occurred?"

"I just told you we went and had a party after the shooting. Does that sound like I felt guilty?"

"You had nightmares."

"They went away after a while."

"There's a notation in your file that you received a reprimand after the shooting incident. What was this about?"

"I got written up for following the FBI manual."

"Please go on."

"It says in the FBI manual that all prisoners must be handcuffed, no matter what the circumstances of the arrest."

"So you handcuffed the man you shot?"

"That's right. If I hadn't, the supervisor at the scene would have written me up for not following procedure."

Dr. Rhodes maintained eye contact with Haynes. "Then what exactly was the dispute concerning the handcuffing of the ... uh ... prisoner?"

"The supervisor said what I did was unbecoming a federal officer."

"Why would he say that?"

"Probably because some of the onlookers in the bank got upset."

"I take it this was because the man you handcuffed was injured?"

"No. It was because he was headless."

"You handcuffed a headless corpse?"

"It was either that or be written up for not following procedure."

Dr. Rhodes stared at the personnel file for a moment, shook his head. "Did you really believe your supervisor would have reprimanded you for failing to handcuff a dead man?"

"Yes."

Dr. Rhodes swallowed a couple of times, reached for his eyeglasses, then stopped himself. He picked up a report, cleared his throat, spoke in a businesslike manner. "This rating report says that you lack initiative, seem constantly 'blue,' and that you have a 'tendency to find fault with everyone and everything.' What is your reaction to these comments?"

Red Haynes gave his right ear a tug. One by one, he cracked each of the knuckles on his right hand by tugging sharply on each finger. "My reaction is that the person who wrote that is a pencil-necked Bureau ass-kisser and a general all-around prick who's not qualified to write an evaluation on anyone."

"Nevertheless, he's someone you have to work with," Dr. Rhodes said.

"Not anymore. He transferred me from the Las Vegas field office to the Organized Crime Strike Force almost ten months ago."

Rhodes flipped the file folder's cover to check the date. He blushed as he noted it. "We are a little behind in consultations."

"The whole government is behind. That's because it has second-rate people working for it. In fact, if you

41

were such a hot-shot psychiatrist you'd be out making big money somewhere, instead of collecting a federal paycheck to work in a chickenshit government clinic."

Dr. Rhodes made a notation in Haynes's file. "I think you are suffering from severe depression, Agent Haynes."

Haynes cracked his knuckles again. The sound was extra-loud, like twigs breaking.

Exasperated, Dr. Rhodes let out his breath. He made notations in the file. "I'm going to recommend that you get into an exercise program...jogging, maybe. When you feel stress coming on I want you to drop whatever you are doing and start jogging."

"I should start the moment I feel stress coming on?"

Dr. Rhodes stopped writing, looked up. "That's right."

Red Haynes came to his feet in a quick-step march. With his bony knees and arms working like pistons he jogged to the door. Keeping his legs moving, he opened the door and jogged directly from the room, through the reception area, and out the front door.

At the federal courthouse, Novak parked the G-car in his assigned spot in the parking lot.

Inside, he took an elevator to the third floor. At the end of a hallway he stopped in front of an unmarked door. He punched numbers on the door's cipher lock. The lock made a snapping sound, and he let himself into a drably decorated room which contained six government-issue desks, some filing cabinets, a radio base station, and a teletype machine. Next to the window was a bulletin board covered with black-and-white photographs—blown-up surveillance shots of Tony Parisi talking to men in casino parking lots.

At an immaculate desk in the corner of the room, Along-for-the-Ride Frank Tyde, a seedy, middle-aged U.S. Customs agent who invariably wore the same brown polyester sport coat and frayed necktie, sat with his feet up on his desk, head turned to face the window, hands behind his head with fingers interlaced, meerschaum pipe jutting from the side of his mouth emitting smoke. It was a position from which he seldom moved. Probably because it would have caused him an unnecessary expenditure of energy, he did not acknowledge Novak's arrival in any way.

John Novak sat down at his desk, rummaged through some paperwork.

"Big day planned, Frank?" Novak said as an aside.

"This afternoon I'll get a haircut, do some shopping at the government store, make a few phone calls around the country to see who's getting promoted... and brief Elliot, our fearless prick of a leader, on an old case. That'll be the hardest part of the day," Tyde said without taking the pipe out of his mouth.

"No overtime planned for today?"

"Already logged in my two hours. I came in early and made some phone calls."

"That sounds like an honest deuce at time-and-a-half," Novak said facetiously. He yanked open a file drawer.

Tyde swung his feet off the desk, ambled to a metal duty-schedule board. He picked up a magnetic metal dot, placed it under his name on a section of the board marked "Sick Leave." "Yes, these long hours can sure take a toll. I'll be taking sick leave tomorrow... to rest up." Then Along-for-the-Ride Tyde's lungs displaced precisely enough air to make a sound that could be recognized as a laugh. Having arranged the duty board, he checked his wristwatch, sat back down at his desk, returned to his pipe-smoking rest position.

Red Haynes shuffled into the room. He looked as if he had been running.

6

"How did it go?" Haynes said to Novak.

Novak smiled proudly. "Bruno went for it."

"The grand jury?" Haynes said.

"We pick him up tomorrow and take him straight to the witness stand."

Haynes extended a hand to his partner. They shook. "This could be the knockout punch for Parisi," he said excitedly. "What made him change his mind?"

"He finally realized there is no other way to go."

"Tomorrow's a long time from now."

"Don't be such a pessimist," Novak said. He walked from the room and down a short hallway to a door with a plastic nameplate which read:

The sound of a television emanated from inside.

Novak knocked on the door. There was the sound of movement, then of the television being turned off. Elliot said, "Come in." Inside, the walls were covered with cheap wooden appreciation plaques of the kind found in most government offices. Elliot, a slender man of Novak's age, sat at an uncluttered desk. Though coatless, he looked preppie-neat in a dark vest, long-sleeved white shirt, and gold collar pin, watch band, and cuff links. He wore eyeglasses with colorless frames and lightly tinted lenses.

"Bruno's ready to take the stand," Novak said.

Elliot raised his eyebrows. "And say what?"

"Everything. How Tony Parisi muscled in at the casinos, how the skim works, who carries it back East. And he knows about the count-room murders, extortion, all of it."

"Sounds real good," Elliot said as a matter of course. "I'll schedule him for next week's grand jury."

"Next week? This isn't just another grand-jury witness," Novak said. "This is the witness who's gonna spill the beans—give us direct evidence on Mr. Big in Las Vegas. I think we should get him on the witness stand immediately before he changes his mind."

"I want to proceed *by the numbers*...make sure that everything is in order before we put him on the witness stand and swear him in."

"I've been playing cat-and-mouse with Bruno for six months to get him to come around," Novak said, straining to keep emotion out of his voice. "The longer we wait, the more chance there is of Parisi finding out that Bruno is a snitch."

"I can understand how you resent taking orders from a

prosecutor like myself. After all, it wasn't your choice to be assigned here."

"If Bruno has a chance to think about it, he'll back out on us."

Elliot drummed his fingers nervously. "I admire the way you've handled this investigation. You've done a fine job. And Washington is going to be overjoyed if we can make a case on Parisi," he said, trying to avoid making a decision.

"I've already made arrangements to meet Bruno, tomorrow morning at the Highland Coffee Shop. He's expecting me to take him directly from there to the grand jury. He wants to get it over with."

In an obvious manner, Elliot checked his wristwatch. He stood up and tucked in his shirt. "I don't want to second-guess you on this," he said as he picked his coat from the coatrack, punched arms into sleeves. "It's your case, and if you feel that strongly about it, we'll put him on the witness stand tomorrow morning. I'm behind you one hundred and fifty percent."

He smiled.

Back in the agents' room, John Novak looked out a window facing the rear of the Golden Nugget Casino. Because it was dusk, there was a glow emanating from the gigantic rooftop neon display, a miner panning for gold. In the distance he could see vehicles whizzing by on the four-lane highway which brought tourists and gambling degenerates into town every day like children hurrying to a birthday party. From the radio base station in the corner of the room came intermittent static and then the sound of an agent on surveillance describing a man who was exiting a vehicle. "...male, white, five-nine, one-fifty..."

Haynes left his desk and joined him at the window. "Did he want to do it *by the numbers?*" Haynes said, mimicking Elliot.

"He agreed to put him in front of the grand jury tomorrow morning," Novak said as he continued to gaze out the window.

Red Haynes moved to his partner, formed his facial muscles into a histrionic Elliot grin. "I'm behind you *one hundred and fifty percent*," he said.

Without taking his pipe out of his mouth, Frank Tyde reached inside a plastic shopping bag that was lying on top of his desk. He removed a white felt baseball cap, placed it firmly on his head. With smoke wafting from the bowl of his pipe, he left his desk, moved past them on his way to the window. Large red letters on the cap read: HAVE A NICE DAY. As Tyde checked himself in the window's reflection, Novak just looked at Haynes and shook his head.

"Don't let the pressure of the job get to ya, Frank," Novak said.

"Oh, I won't."

The next morning, Red Haynes, dressed for work, sat at the dinette table. His wife, Martha, a tiny woman who shunned makeup and fashionable attire for sweat shirts and jeans, stood at the stove. He stared out the window at his front yard—a patch of grass which was exactly the same size as all the others in the tract. As Martha refilled his coffee cup, his scornful teenage sons, both gangly and burdened with their ever-present athletic gear, stormed through the kitchen grabbing toast, gulping milk.

The car started and they sped off. Red Haynes stifled the urge to scream out the window at them to slow down. Martha returned the coffeepot to the stove.

"What kind of a case are you going to work on today?"

"Who cares?"

"You're doing it again."

"Whatsat?" he said as if he didn't understand what she was talking about.

Martha sat down at the table. She mixed cream into her coffee. "You're just sitting there and staring. The doctor said it was better for you to talk about the job ... to share things."

"That's what shrinks get paid to say."

In a gesture of frustration, Martha let out her breath.

"With that attitude you're going to stay depressed. The doctor told you that."

"He said I'm suffering from job burnout. Can you imagine that the government pays him good money for that?"

A car pulled up outside. It was Novak.

Haynes stood up, lifted his shapeless suitcoat off the back of the chair. As he moved to the door, Martha hurried to a cupboard and took out a small bottle of pills. At the door, she held the bottle out to him. Red Haynes shook his head as if she were trying to hand him poison. He leaned down and gave her a kiss.

"The doctor said you should take these."

"All doctors are assholes," Red Haynes said on his way out the door.

A few minutes later, Novak steered into the parking lot of the Highland Coffee Shop. He cruised past rows of cars in the crowded lot until he found Bruno's, parked in the corner. It was empty. "He must be having coffee," Haynes said. "Should I go inside and let him know we're here?"

Novak checked his wristwatch. "Let him come out on his own."

Inside the restaurant, Bruno Santoro was seated at the counter. Having noticed Novak's car, he tugged the sleeve of his sport coat, checked his Rolex. Leaving a breakfast he had ordered but was too nervous to eat, he stood and moved closer to the window. Novak and Haynes were parked at the edge of the lot. At an unmanned cash register, he left enough money to pay his bill, then headed for the door. As he reached it, he stopped for a moment and took a few deep breaths. For the hundredth time he considered whether he should just tell Novak he had changed his mind about testifying. "I can't do it," he pictured himself saying. In his mind, Novak just shook his head and drove off, leaving him alone in the parking lot.

Then, because he knew if he didn't testify he would

end up going to prison, Bruno Santoro shoved open the door and moved directly across the parking lot to his Cadillac. He opened the driver's door and climbed in, tugged the headlight switch as a signal to Novak. The headlights of Novak's car flashed twice. Bruno Santoro removed keys from the pocket of his coat. As he shoved a key into the ignition, there was a sound like that of a clothespin snapping shut, then a buzzing.

"No!" he screamed, scrambling to open the driver's door. As his left foot touched the pavement there was a blinding explosion and Bruno Santoro felt a thousand-horsepower piledriver pierce the floorboard of the car and slam his balls and pecker through his body and out the top of his head.

The explosion, which had lifted the Cadillac fully off the ground, snapped Novak's head backward and made his ears ring. Stunned, he hoisted himself out of the G-car. Followed by Haynes, he ran toward the billowing flame and smoke...and stopped. The force of the blast had torn the roof open and transformed the vehicle into two twisted pieces of metal. The air was filled with an odor that reminded Novak of Vietnam.

An out-of-breath Haynes almost fell. "Goddam. *Goddam!*"

John Novak suddenly realized that besides fragments of auto metal and upholstery, the parking lot around him was also covered with white-and-pink pieces of human matter. He started to speak and found he couldn't. He cleared his throat. "Block off the entrance to the lot, Red," he said without taking his eyes off the smoldering wreckage.

He willed himself to feel nothing.

It didn't work.

7 Eddie had been on Monica's mind since she'd climbed out of bed. With the windows rolled up and the air conditioning on, she drove her silver Porsche 911 slowly down Las Vegas Boulevard past the Silver Dollar Motel, a cheaply built thirty-rooms-and-pool which looked like hundreds of others in the city; this place catered to gamblers down on their luck, hookers, transient crooks, and poor tourists who preferred to spend their money on the slot machines rather than a deluxe room at one of the luxury hotel/casinos. Noting that there were no suspicious-looking cars in the area (she knew cops loved to use such places to set traps), she pulled into the crowded parking lot and, to make sure a nosy motel manager couldn't take down her license plate, parked away from the registration office.

Having checked her platinum coiffure in the rearview mirror, she climbed out of the sports car and strutted past a swimming pool in which a couple of Styrofoam cups floated to a room on the ground floor. She looked around again, knocked softly.

"Who's there?" said a man with a British accent.

"Monica."

The door was opened by a bearded, overweight man wearing a Hawaiian shirt and gold chains. "Long time no see," he said. He glanced about suspiciously, then invited her in.

"I prefer to talk out here," she said, moving toward the pool.

"What, you afraid of me?"

"Please don't be difficult, Leo. I'm in a hurry."

Leo shook his head and stepped out of the room. He closed the door behind him, followed her to the pool. "I don't know what you're so worried about. We've done business before."

"Then you should know that's just the way I am," she said as she sat down in a deck chair.

"If you're looking for some more of those stock certificates, you're too late. I already unloaded 'em."

"Stock certificates are shit, Leo."

"So don't buy 'em."

"I'm looking for something I can turn quickly."

Leo sat down on a deck chair next to her. "I have some cashier's checks . . . credit cards . . ."

She shook her head. "How about some of those nice chips that have been hitting the street?"

Leo took out a package of chewing gum from his shirt pocket. He unwrapped a stick. "Who told you about those?" he said as he placed the stick of gum in his mouth.

"What the hell's the difference who told me?"

"So I'm a little paranoid. That's how I keep out of jail."

She stood up. "If you don't trust me, then I don't trust you, you son of a bitch." They stared at one another for a moment, then she turned to walk away.

"What kind of a deal are you thinking about?"

She stopped walking, turned to face him. "I'm not thinking about anything until I see a sample," she said.

He looked both ways, then reached into his breast pocket. He pulled out a pale blue gaming chip and tossed it to her. She caught it. It was a hundred-dollar chip, and the round label in the center bore the spaceship logo of the Stardust Casino. She turned it over. The other side was the same. As far as she was concerned, the chip might as well have been real.

"You like?"

"I like."

"The price is fifty percent."

"Nothing sells for fifty percent, Leo."

"So talk to me."

"I could take a lot of it at ten points. But I can't go higher."

"Then we can't do business. Hell, I'll pass the shit myself before I unload it at ten points."

"Is it your stuff?"

"I'm just a middleman."

She tossed the chip. He caught it. "Did anyone ever tell you you'd look a lot better without a beard?" she said.

For a moment, Leo just sat there staring at her. As she turned and strutted toward her car, she heard him rise from the deck chair. "I got people waiting in line for this shit," he said. "You can have it for twenty percent if you can take at least a hundred grand worth."

"Fuck you, Leo," Monica said as she opened the door of the Porsche. She climbed in and drove off.

Later, back at her spacious air-conditioned apartment, Monica still couldn't get Eddie off her mind. Lying on the sofa, wearing only a black bra and panties, she looked up from the *Wall Street Journal* and faced her reflection in the decorative mirrored tiles which covered the ceiling. It occurred to her that her black underwear contrasted nicely with her platinum-blondness.

Her living room was decorated with what she liked to think was a sense of organization: cypress-paneled walls, a Shaker rocker, wood-and-rush chairs, and no pattern in either the azure carpet or the upholstery. A wall drama composed of reproductions of American artifacts, including a horse-and-surrey weathervane and a cigar-store Indian, was the focus of the room. Though she had no real affinity for such items, she relished the sense of nostalgia they created.

All in all, as she often said to herself, the apartment was the perfect front.

She removed the eyeglasses which she never wore in public, folded the newspaper, and tossed it onto a coffee table on which five telephones rested. For a moment she just lay there and considered whether she should get dressed and eat lunch in one of the restaurants on the Strip (Caesars Palace was her favorite), or masturbate, or take a swim in the pool. Before she could decide, one of the phones rang. She picked up the receiver.

"Investment Associates," she said. "Monica Atwood speaking."

"This is the answering service," a woman said. "You have six calls from that man in Utah. He's still screaming about his money and says you never return his calls."

"The next time he calls tell him I'm in...Saudi Arabia. You don't know when I'll be back." As she set the phone down, another phone rang. She picked it up. "Nevada Gold Mining Trust," she said. "Monica Butler speaking."

"This is Mrs. Dorchester," said a woman in a feeble voice. "I think I should wait before I invest. I'm just not sure."

"I was just going to call you," Monica said. "The mine started back into operation this morning, and the first assay was positive. A team of executives from IBM is en route from New York at this very moment. It looks like they are going to make an offer for the entire mining conglomerate later in the day. It may be too late for small investors anyway."

"Oh," said the woman hesitantly. "I just wonder what I should do."

"If you can send me a money order for six hundred, I'll try to place a hold order on a stock option. That way even if IBM buys the mine you'd be guaranteed to at least double your money within sixty days. But I can't allow you to send any more than six hundred. I have to share the opportunity with my other clients."

"Should I send the money to your post-office box?"

"That's right...and I've gotta run. The assay people are here."

"Well, uh, thank you," Mrs. Dorchester said as Monica set the receiver down.

She stood up and strutted across thick shag carpeting into the bedroom. At the mirror, she removed her brassiere, stuck her chest out. Great nips, if she did say so herself. Standing there, her platinum hair a mess and her face devoid of makeup, she decided how she would kill the rest of the day. She would do her nails, check her post-office box, pay her telephone bill, and perhaps smoke a joint.

But first, she said to herself as she pulled down her panties, it was time to do something strictly for herself.

8 John Novak sat with Elliot at a table to the right of the witness stand.

The federal grand jury's hearing room, a starkly decorated chamber with high, polished wooden doors, was on the top floor of the federal courthouse. It was only nine o'clock but already, because of the temperature outside, the air conditioner was on in the room. Next to the witness stand was a large easel on which were blown-up color photographs: the wreckage of Bruno Santoro's car, and a morgue photo of a coroner's deputy pointing at what was left of Bruno's body.

Novak thought the grand jurors, sixteen middle-class men and women fidgeting in high-backed swivel chairs, looked less bored than usual. And the stenotypist, an oriental man with thick glasses, was sitting up in his chair rather than slouching as he normally did. They always perked up with well-known witnesses.

The foreman of the grand jury, a well-dressed, gray-haired man who looked as if he used pomade, rapped his knuckles on the long table in front of him to get the attention of the group. Talking subsided. "The Grand Jury for the Southern District of Nevada calls Anthony Parisi." He nodded to a younger man sitting near the door.

The man stood up, opened the door. "Please step in, Mr. Parisi," he said.

Tony Parisi, fortyish, well fed, well groomed, dark, and wearing a gray silk necktie and charcoal suit tailored to hide his paunch, entered the room. The man showed him to the witness stand. Having been sworn in by the jury foreman, he sat down.

Elliot stood up. "Please state your full name."

"Anthony Salvatore Parisi."

"Mr. Parisi, be advised that you are before the United States Grand Jury for the Southern District of Nevada. For the record, I am Ronald Elliot, attorney-in-charge of the Department of Justice Strike Force Against Organized Crime and Racketeering. Do you understand that, sir?"

"Yes."

"I am going to ask you a number of questions concerning a matter that this federal grand jury has chosen to investigate. You have the right to consult with an attorney before answering any of these questions. Do you understand that, sir?"

"Yes."

"Have you ever had the occasion to meet one Bruno Santoro?"

Parisi reached into his breast pocket, removed a piece of paper. He unfolded it. "On advice of counsel I respectfully refuse to answer that question on the grounds of the Fifth Amendment of the Constitution of the United States in that any answer I may give could tend to incriminate me." He set the paper down on the witness stand.

Elliot looked at Novak, then at the foreman of the grand jury. He cleared his throat. "Mr. Parisi, are you a member of the Vacarillo crime family?"

Parisi picked up the paper. "On advice of counsel I respectfully..."

Novak bit his lip. He sat there for the next hour as Parisi read the statement over and over again in answer to Elliot's questions. The members of the grand jury began to slouch in their chairs, tip back and forth, yawn.

When the hearing was finally over and the grand jury was adjourned, Novak followed Parisi out of the hearing room and down a long hallway to an elevator bank. Parisi pressed the button. There was no one else in the hallway.

"Bruno told me your name isn't shit on the street," Novak said in a low tone.

Parisi glared at him.

"The word is the people back East think you're just a flash in the pan," Novak said. "They're waiting for you to make a mistake out here."

"I got nothing to say to you."

"Novak's the name...John Novak. I'm coming for you."

"You're coming for me?" Parisi asked sarcastically.

"That's right," Novak said. "I'm the one who's gonna lock you up." He smiled.

The elevator doors opened.

"Fuck you," Parisi said.

Novak winked.

Parisi, still glaring, stepped onto the elevator. The elevator doors closed. Novak stopped smiling.

Elliot approached, carrying the stack of legal papers he had had with him in the grand-jury room. "We can force him to testify with a grant of immunity. But if we do that, we can never prosecute him for any crime he testifies about. He's got us on a Ferris wheel."

"Until I recruit another informant."

"Considering the luck you've...uh...we've had with

informants, maybe it's better to approach Parisi from another angle."

"Like what?"

"A month or so from now we could call some of his friends before the grand jury again. Make him sweat."

"They'll just take the Fifth like he did."

"If we do this *by the numbers* we can keep him guessing, keep his organization in turmoil, until we get an opening."

"I'd rather put him in prison than play the bluff game," Novak said.

"If you can figure a way to do just that, please let me know," Elliot said. He hurried toward an elevator.

Eddie Sands awoke early. He flipped his prison blanket onto the cement floor, scrambled out of his bunk as if out of a grave. He shaved and dressed. Immediately he began packing his possessions: a box of cheap stationery, a fountain pen, some paperback books (*The Art of Playing Craps, Inside the Mafia,* James Jones's *From Here to Eternity*), and a hardcover titled *My Way in American Free Enterprise* by Harry Desmond, the one-time evangelist turned born-again flag-waving self-serving conglomerateur, a darling of the media who, Sands figured, was probably a ruthless prick and confidence man. He managed to fit all the items as well as a thick stack of letters from Monica into a brown paper sack. Because he was too keyed up to sit down, he stood at the cell door until breakfast time, when the door opened automatically.

It was noon by the time he was allowed to pass the last guard station and walk out the front door of the prison. Outside, as he marched across the parking lot and directly down Ferry Street, he felt a tingling sensation spread across his back, neck, and face. Then suddenly he was jogging—*jogging away from the joint!* By the time he reached the sedan he was out of breath. He replaced the license plates, then climbed in, started the engine, and headed toward the freeway. As he wound from freeway to freeway across Los Angeles toward the Cajon Pass, he imagined, just as he had every night in his cell, the various ways he would fuck Monica when he was finally with her again.

Four hours later, as Sands neared the outskirts of Las Vegas, his rearview mirror was suddenly filled with the reflection of a police car's blinking red light. Holding his breath, he slowed down and pulled to the right shoulder of the road.

As he came to a complete stop, his eyes were riveted to the rearview mirror. A uniformed officer, a tall man with weathered features, lumbered out of the police car and put on his hat. Sands breathed an audible sigh of relief. He climbed out of the sedan and moved quickly toward the officer. Smiling, he offered his hand. "Eddie Sands," he said. "I used to be on the job—Detective Bureau, Organized Crime Intelligence."

"Haven't seen you since...uh," the officer said as they shook hands.

"Since I was fired from the department," Sands said, taking note of the officer's name tag—Fisher.

The officer, ill at ease, bit his lip. "What are you up to these days?" he said.

"I'm a private investigator...making lots of bucks," Sands said, maintaining his smile.

"I never believed any of that stuff I read in the papers about you."

"Thanks, buddy," Sands said as he gave the officer a friendly punch on the shoulder.

"Try to slow it down a little," the officer said on his way back to the squad car.

Sands gave a little salute. "You betcha," he said. As he climbed back into the sedan, the police car sped by.

A few minutes later, Eddie Sands cruised onto the Las Vegas Strip, a desert mirage of monstrous signboards, casino facades, and million-watt neon marquees which, to him, seemed alive and inviting.

He was back in his town—the city of lights, tights, and prize fights, pointy-titted showgirls, maître d's with the slickest palms west of the Mississippi, gamblers who wore Stetson hats, whores who looked like movie stars, professional stick men, fixers, pickpockets, keno addicts, gallery spies, confidence men from all parts of the world, businessmen and their girlfriends in for the weekend, amateur and professional card counters, dice mechanics, and all manner of stage entertainers, those at the top of the show-biz circuit and those on their way down the drain.

As Sands knocked on Monica's door, he felt excitement well in his loins. He could feel himself becoming uncontrollably erect, like a teenager. Finally, she opened the door. They threw arms around each other. As their lips and tongues met he was enveloped in the scent of her perfume, the softness of her hair. They tore at each other's clothing. Naked, they dropped onto the plush carpet and fucked with abandon. Monica used her palms to wipe perspiration from Sands's brow as he concentrated like a yogi on not ejaculating. Finally, he moaned and gave in to what was perhaps the most powerful orgasm of his life. Neither tired nor spent, he pulled her to her feet and led her into the bedroom. There he lay on the bed. She climbed on top of him. As he massaged her breasts roughly, they screwed again until they were both completely exhausted.

"Goddam, I missed you," she said.

"Don't talk about it."

She kissed him on the cheek and reached to the nightstand for a package of cigarettes. "Was Bruce O'Hara easy?"

"Nobody is easy."

"Where are you taking me for dinner?" she said.

"Caesars Palace. Nothing is too good for you, fast-talking lady."

9 Later that evening Eddie Sands sat with Monica in a dimly lit private booth at Caesars Palace. They talked softly, paying no attention to the tuxedoed waiters who weaved expertly among gold-leafed Roman columns carrying flaming dishes, or the piped-in violin music mixing with the sound of jackpot bells and slot machines from the casino floor below.

A young olive-complexioned waiter brought a standing ice bucket to their table. Having twirled a bottle of Dom Pérignon in the ice and filled their glasses, he hurried away.

Eddie Sands raised a toast. "Here's to you and me," he said. She moved closer to him in the booth.

"May I ask you a question?"

"Sure."

"When you were on the police department, how did you first get started with Tony?"

"I was investigating him—following him all day and writing bullshit surveillance reports. We got to know each other."

"The same way you met me."

Eddie Sands shook his head. "Not really. At the time no one could figure out what Tony was up to, how he was making all his money. But there was no doubt about you. I had a stack of complaints on you."

"The first time you interviewed me I was shaking like a leaf. Did you notice?"

Eddie Sands shook his head. "You were smooth."

"You were smooth, too," she said. "Too smooth for a cop."

"How so?"

"You would stare at my tits, look up, smile, then ask me a question. It was unnerving. But I could tell that if I did what you wanted, you wouldn't take me to jail."

He leaned toward her. They kissed. Eddie Sands picked up his glass, took a sip.

"You didn't think I'd be here when you got out, did you?" Monica said.

"I had my doubts," he said after a while.

"When I love somebody, I really love 'em."

"I love you too, baby."

The waiters brought their meal in leisurely courses: escargots, lobster thermidor, a dessert of baked Alaska. Perhaps it was during the dessert that Eddie Sands began to feel as if his conviction and prison sentence hadn't really occurred, as if it were just another distasteful police experience—like finding a swollen corpse along the roadway or having to beat some drunken moron into submission, an event that recurred in one's memory for a while and then, for the sake of sanity, flickered into the garbage can of the mind.

After dinner they stopped downstairs in the casino. Sands watched the action at a crap table as mesmerized gamblers took turns rolling the dice. Then, having wandered through the casino crowd, they made their way to the parking lot.

The car windows were open on the way back to Monica's place, and Eddie Sands felt as if the crisp desert breeze on his face was cleansing his mind of the gray prison haze. He steered along a block lined with pawnshops and wedding chapels and onto the highway.

Monica turned to him. "Now that you're out, what are we gonna do?" she said.

"We're gonna make money. Enough money to get over...once and for all."

Monica's eyes returned to the road. "I guess that's about it."

"And get married," he said. "It's you and me from here on in, fast-talking lady. You're all I've got."

Without meeting his gaze, Monica slid closer to him and put her head on his shoulder. As she clutched his right arm tightly, he could feel the softness of her breasts.

Back at her apartment, they hurried into the bedroom and made love again. Afterward, lying with arms around her, Eddie Sands could feel Monica's heart beating, her abdomen gently meeting his with each breath.

"I wish you hadn't gone to Tony Parisi in order to get out," she said.

"He was the only one with a connection to the Federal Parole Board. It was either go to him or do the rest of my time."

"But now he owns you."

"Nobody owns me, babe."

"Tony is dangerous. He can have anything done in this town. He just had the Corcoran brothers blow up Bruno Santoro."

"Lemme tell you something, babe. I am...uh, I *was* a cop. So hoods don't scare me. And Tony Parisi is nothing but a New York tenement-house meatball who made good. Fuck him and the Corcoran brothers."

"I'd rather fuck you," she whispered as she reached between his legs.

The next day, Eddie Sands drove slowly along the Strip, turning off here and there to wind his way along side streets he knew like the back of his hand. There was no corner in town that didn't carry some memory— a foot pursuit in the parking lot of the Sahara, a shoot-out with robbers at the Nevada National Bank on Tropicana Boulevard, three screaming whores in an all-out fight in front of the Showboat Motel.

Finally he pulled into a gigantic parking lot which surrounded the Stardust Hotel and Casino, an expansive, gaudy building with enormous neon arches criss-crossing a multidoored entrance. He parked the car. Having removed the briefcase containing the fifty thousand dollars from the trunk, he carried it across the parking lot and up the imitation-marble steps. He strolled through the automatic doors. Engulfed in the familiar whir of slot machines, the smell of cigarette smoke and air-conditioned coolness, he just stood there for a moment and savored the fact that he was a free man.

As he weaved his way through the crowd of busy slot players he had the strange feeling, which he attributed to having been in prison, that he was invisible. And he saw the "carpet joint" for what it was—an institution designed with neither windows, doors, chairs, nor wall clocks in order to mesmerize the tourists therein trapped into losing track of time and place as they squandered money. He understood this, and he felt at home.

In the less-than-crowded bar, he approached the bartender, a slim effeminate man who smiled, stealing a glance at Sands's groin.

"I'm here to see Tony," Sands said.

"Does he know you?"

"Just tell him Eddie Sands is here," Sands said.

The bartender made a brief phone call.

A few minutes later, a tall man with a grayish Mediterranean complexion and a large purple birthmark on his neck approached. He wore a black Italian-cut sport coat. "I'm Vito Fanducci," he said. "Tony's upstairs."

They took an elevator to the penthouse level, where Vito led Sands to a suite at the end of the hallway. He used a key to open the door, motioned Sands into the room. "Tony wants you to wait for him in here."

Sands entered, and Vito closed the door behind him. The room was expansive, airy, furnished with white Danish-modern sofas and chairs.

Sands strolled across the room to a wall of glass doors which led onto a balcony overlooking the northern end of the Las Vegas Strip. Having taken in the view, he set his briefcase down on a portable bar in the corner of the room and picked up a newspaper. In the Metropolitan section of the paper he read a six-column article captioned "Feds Probe Alleged Skimming at Three Casinos." At the sound of a key slipping into the front door, he set the paper down.

Tony Parisi, his paunch accentuated by a tight-fitting golf shirt, stepped in the front door. He wore beltless checkered trousers, and his ever-present handful of cigars bulged from his shirt pocket.

They met in the middle of the room in an insincere *abrazo*. "Been laid yet?" Parisi asked, giving Sands a slug on the shoulder as he made his way to the bar.

"What's that have to do with anything?" Sands said.

"The day I got out of TI I had a broad waiting," Parisi said. "Porked her right there in the backseat of the car in the prison parking lot." He poured whiskey over ice. "When I came it was like my balls were shooting out of the end of my cock." He chuckled.

"Nice," Sands said. He picked up his drink.

Parisi came from behind the bar, clinked his glass to Sands's. "Welcome back," he said. As they drank, Sands noticed that Parisi barely touched the glass to his lips. Instead, he set his drink down, unsnapped the hinge locks on the briefcase, opened the lid.

"I pushed for more," Sands said. "But fifty was all the man would go. He was tough. Real tough."

"How could a guy who's into that kind of shit be *tough?*" Parisi said. He thumbed some of the bills.

Sands smiled wryly. "You just answered your own question," he said.

Realizing that the comment was meant to be humorous, Parisi forced a smile, then a laugh. "That's right. To get a charge out of having hat pins stuck through your nuts you gotta be a tough monkey." He yanked a cigar out of his shirt pocket, and with a ratlike bite, offed the end, then spit it onto the carpet. "The juice I have with the Federal Parole Board is new. One of those deals where I get to a guy from Newark who knows a lawyer who knows a Congressman who knows bleepety bleepety bleep. I'm not keeping a dime of the fifty for myself."

"I hear you've been doing real well," Sands said, not bothering to say thanks. He figured Parisi was bullshitting him about the money.

"Real well was the way it *used* to be in this town. When we owned the casinos we didn't have to worry about collecting a little taste here and there. The countroom people, the casino managers, the pit bosses...we was all one big happy family. The biggest problem was finding somebody to drive the skim money back East every week." He licked the end of his cigar, then looked at it. "The way the casinos are now, you gotta crack heads to make a buck. You gotta spill blood before they believe you."

Sands shook his head as if he really gave a shit.

"Television."

"Television?" Sands said.

"I pay a visit to one of the casino people. I lay the touch on them real nice-like. I tell them I'm their new partner. But they don't get it. They think it's like something they see on TV. They think everything is gonna work out okay even if they don't send me my weekly piece. Just like things work out okay at the end of a TV show." Parisi made a face as he took three big puffs from the cigar, making the ash glow. "So people get clipped."

"How are the cops?"

"I change rooms a lot, go from place to place to keep 'em guessing. And I get a call if anything big is happening." Parisi stepped out onto the balcony, blew smoke at Las Vegas. "Can he be had twice?" he said.

"You're talking about a rehash."

"That's right—going right back to the motherfucker and doing him again."

"He might blow."

"The man thinks he's in a cross—otherwise he wouldn't have sprung like he did," Parisi said.

"I guess I could try it," Sands said.

Parisi turned to face him. "I know you can do it. Say we go fifty-fifty on the take?"

"Sounds fair enough," Sands said, though it didn't.

Eddie Sands wandered toward the door.

"Tell me something," Parisi said in a voice loud enough so he could be heard from across the room. Sands turned.

"With only six months to go on work release, why didn't you just save the fifty K and serve out your time?"

Without acknowledging the question, Sands left the room.

 Standing on the balcony of a room at the Stardust, John Novak, dressed in slacks and a loose-flowing sport shirt that covered his gun, lit another cigarette. As he crushed the empty package he told himself he'd been smoking too much. But he always smoked too much on surveillances.

"What are they talking about?" he said.

Red Haynes, wearing earphones that looked small because of the size of his ears, adjusted the volume control on a briefcase-size receiver which was sitting on the dressing table in front of him. "The guy Parisi's talking to sounds like a confidence man...and he might have just been released from Terminal Island...was on work release when he got out. Small talk."

"We've been sitting here for five days and Parisi hasn't said a word to anyone about the bombing," Novak said, thinking out loud.

Suddenly, Haynes's hands cupped the earphones. "The visitor is leaving," he said.

Novak hurried to the door and put an eye to the peep-hole. A pale, clean-featured man with neat, close-cropped hair came out of the door across the hall and headed toward an elevator bank. Quietly, Novak turned the door handle. He stepped out of the room and moved down the hall. With the sound of a chime, the elevator arrived. Novak followed the man into the elevator. As the man pressed a button marked "Lobby/Casino," Novak feigned reaching for the same button and notic-ing that it was already lit. The doors closed. Casually, the man glanced at his wristwatch, then at Novak. The elevator descended as Novak, avoiding direct eye con-tact as the man stared at him, lifted his eyes to the row of blinking numbers above the door.

Finally, the doors opened onto the bustling, smoky ca-sino. Novak allowed the man to step out first. The man moved directly into a slot-machine area which was crowded with busy players and sallow-faced change girls in fishnet stockings. Novak followed at a discreet distance.

Suddenly, a group of Japanese tourists, clustered around an oversized slot machine, engulfed him, and Novak realized that he had lost sight of the man. He looked about in the casino, then hurried outside onto the crowded taxi-lined sidewalk of Las Vegas Boule-vard. The man was gone.

"Shit," Novak said out loud. Then he turned and walked quickly to the driveway exit. Blending in with a crowd of people waiting for taxis, he surveyed the driver of every vehicle leaving the parking lot. About ten minutes later, the man who had been in Parisi's room drove out in a Chevrolet sedan. Novak yanked a ballpoint pen from his shirt pocket and scribbled the license number of the Chevy on the palm of his hand. It was a California plate.

When Novak returned to the room, Red Haynes was still sitting in front of the tape recorder. He looked up.

"He left in a Chevy."

"Get the license plate?"

Novak held up his ink-marked palm. He copied the license number onto a page in his investigative notebook, then stepped into the bathroom and washed his hands.

Haynes's fingertips touched his earphones. "Parisi's telling the hotel operator not to put any calls through to the room....Now he's brushing his teeth." He removed the earphones and dropped them on the dressing table. "It's time for the asshole to take his daily nap."

Novak asked to hear the last conversation. Haynes nodded. He pressed the rewind button on the machine, stood up, and stretched. The tape rewound, he hit the play button. As the tape began to play, Haynes moved about in the room shadow boxing, like some skinny-assed boxer before a fight.

Novak sat down in front of the tape recorder and made notes on a pad of hotel stationery. Finally, he turned the machine off.

Standing in front of the balcony, Red Haynes cracked his knuckles one by one. "Whaddaya make of it?" he said.

Novak rubbed his chin as he looked at his notes. He had written "fifty grand" and "six months to go."

"Five days' work, and we end up with a reel of tape full of small talk: Parisi and some local hoods, Parisi and his girlfriend, Parisi and his foul-mouthed sister in San Francisco, Parisi and some con just out of the joint... and not one word about Bruno getting blown up," Haynes said. "Practically a whole week shot."

As Novak struck a match to light a cigarette, it came to him.

"So where do we go from here?" Red Haynes said.

But Novak was reliving his last conversation with Bruno Santoro, and he only half-heard the question. Absentmindedly, he blew out the flame.

Later, at the Las Vegas Racquetball Club, Novak changed into athletic trunks, T-shirt, and court shoes. He left the locker room, headed down a wide, carpeted hallway which was filled with the muffled sound of racquetballs bouncing off court walls. He stopped at the door near the end of the hall, peered through a glass peephole. Lorraine Traynor, attired in trunks and a loose-fitting T-shirt, was standing in the middle of the court facing the front wall. Gripping her racquet firmly, she gave the ball a bounce, then, with a practiced swing, fired it low against the front wall. A kill shot. Novak opened the door and stepped inside.

"Sorry I'm late," he said.

"How did the bugging go?"

"Parisi didn't say anything definite. Not a word that could tie him to the bombing."

She whacked another shot at the wall. As it bounced toward the back wall Novak made a powerful return.

"So of course you want the authorized time on the bug order extended," Lorraine said as she tapped the ball lightly. It hit the front wall low and dribbled back.

"If you don't mind."

"How do you justify it?" she said.

"Just because he didn't come right out and say he had Bruno killed during the time we were listening doesn't mean he's innocent."

"The defense would say that if you listened to Parisi's conversations for five days and he didn't say a word about the bombing, what makes you think that listening to him for another five days, or five years for that matter, would yield any different results?"

"What do I care what a defense attorney might say?" Novak said as he moved across the court. He reached down, picked up the ball.

"I can't extend the eavesdroppng order without some proof that you're not just on a fishing expedition for evidence."

Novak shook his head. "Anyone listening to the tape would know that the man is a crook."

"Under the Constitution, even crooks have the right to privacy. Go ahead and serve."

Novak moved forward to the service line. He bounced the ball a couple of times. "Where does it say that?" he said. Then, with a powerful swing, he slammed the ball. It hit the front wall like a shot.

Just south of the Desert Inn, Eddie Sands turned off Las Vegas Boulevard onto a side street. Halfway down the block, situated between a pair of cheapie hotels, was the Plush Pony Cocktail Lounge, which the vice cops had always called the Dog because of the misshapen neon pony above the door and the looks of the women who hung out in the place. Sands parked in front and went in.

Inside the dimly lit bar, things were as he remembered them—black leather booths and a large, comfortable bar. The ten or so male customers at the bar looked like bookmakers and collectors rather than tourists.

Ray Beadle, a husky man with a crew cut who was a few years older than Sands, sat at the bar facing the door. He spotted Sands, hurried to him, grabbed his hand in a friendship lock, slapped him on the back. "Good to see you back, partner." Sands noticed that Beadle was wearing the same brown sport coat he had worn before Sands had gone to prison.

"Gonna buy me a drink?" Sands said.

"Absolutely."

Sands motioned to a booth away from the others. Beadle stared at him for a moment, then followed. They sat down.

"I owe you, partner," Beadle said. "You could have done yourself a lot of good by handing me up to internal affairs."

"I told you that if I ever had to walk, I'd walk alone."

"You're a man of your word."

"On the other hand, now I wish I'd ratted on you," Sands said with a hint of a smile. "I could have used the company."

They looked at each other for a moment. Sands laughed. Beadle, looking uncomfortable, laughed along.

"How'd you get out?"

"I paid the price."

"Who handled it?"

"Tony Parisi."

"That's the least he coulda done for you," Beadle said.

"I hear Tony is now the man to see in this town."

"It all happened right after you went in. Tony got real big."

"How did he do it?" Sands said.

"He cracked a few coconuts, iced a couple count-room guys, and the casino owners shitted out and let him have his way. He does business in one casino for a while and then moves on. They all give him a taste. A joke, isn't it?"

Eddie Sands shrugged. "In the old days a guy like Parisi would try to muscle in at one of the big places and he'd find himself out in the desert with a coyote eating his ass for dinner."

"The big guys from Cleveland and Chicago sold to the big corporations," Beadle said. "They got yuppies running the places now."

Sands slapped his old friend on the shoulder. "How are ya makin' it these days?"

"My sorry ass makes enough to get by. I collect a few debts for the bookies...that plus my police pension."

A knock-kneed waitress wearing a short white fringed buckskin skirt and purple lipstick came to the table.

"Can I get you fellas something?" she said in a Southern drawl. Beadle introduced her as Tex. They ordered drinks. As Tex walked away, Sands admired the way she moved her hips.

"Nice broad, but don't even think about it," Beadle said. "I've been to her apartment. Dirty clothes, empty Kotex boxes, full trash baskets, cats crawling on the kitchen table. To me a dirty apartment means a dirty box. I'd expect gnats and blowflies to come flying out of her pussy. She'd invited me over, but I left without balling her sorry ass."

"I'm not interested anyway."

"You gonna marry Monica?"

Sands nodded. "And you're gonna be the best man.

73

But first I have some business to take care of. That's why I stopped by to see you."

Ray Beadle swallowed twice. "What kind of business?"

"The touch-play business...like the old days when you and I worked the vice squad. I need a backup man."

Ray Beadle examined the palms of his hands. "Extortion is a heavy beef."

"It's also where the heavy gold is."

"How much are we talking about?"

"I just took somebody down for fifty. With a backup man I can make a return trip."

Tex, with buckskin flapping, brought drinks to the table. As she set the drinks down, Sands noticed that she had dirty fingernails. She winked, moved back to the bar.

Ray Beadle, with furrowed brow, fingered the moisture on the outside of his cocktail glass. Then he picked up the glass, took a big drink, wiped his mouth with the back of his hand. "I can't do time," he said. "My sorry ass just ain't made to do time."

"There's a lot of bucks to be made," Sands said.

"Easier said than done."

"I guess you could say that about anything."

"You haven't changed a bit, Eddie."

"Yes I have. I've changed into a guy that's headed for the five-dollar tables rather than the slot machines. I'm through being a stooge for the police department or Parisi or anyone else." Eddie Sands drained the vodka from his glass. His lips burned.

"Ain't this a bitch. You and me sitting here on our sorry asses talking shit...just like old times."

"Are we still a team?" Sands said.

"Come to think of it, that sorry-assed pension check of mine doesn't go very far in this goddam town... partner."

11

It was seven in the morning and every seat on the flight to L.A. was filled. The passengers, Eddie Sands thought, looked tired and hungover, and had that forlorn expression peculiar to gamblers and losers.

During the short flight, Sands and Ray Beadle, both dressed in suits and ties, talked mostly of their years on the police department: the time they bugged the room of a New Jersey hood and overheard him in a spirited session of anal sex with a young male prostitute; the time they got so drunk at a police retirement party that when they left they couldn't find their police sedan in a crowded casino parking lot. Cop talk.

Once in L.A., having rented a car with a cash deposit, Sands steered out of the airport road and onto a freeway heading north. He noticed that Beadle kept rubbing his hands nervously on his pant legs.

"What happens if this sorry-assed motherfucker just flat freaks out and calls the cops?" Beadle said.

Sands smiled. "Why would he want to do that?" he said calmly.

"Don't fuck with me like that, partner. Anything can happen. You know that."

Sands kept on driving.

"Did you hear what I said?"

"Relax."

At Sunset Boulevard, Sands steered off the freeway and headed east a few miles along the northern edge of the sprawling UCLA campus, then down into a Beverly Hills residential area. Even though he'd been there only once, Sands was able to find Bruce O'Hara's home without a single wrong turn.

He glanced at Ray Beadle, who looked slightly pale, and knocked loudly on the door. His heart was pounding. There was the sound of footsteps. The door opened. Bruce O'Hara was dressed in a red jogging suit.

"I'm sorry to bother you so early, Mr. O'Hara," Sands said.

O'Hara's gaze moved slowly from Sands to Beadle.

"This is Captain Powers," Sands said politely. "He's in charge of the department's Detective Bureau. He asked to speak with you." Beadle nodded.

The movie star glared at Sands. "You told me this was resolved."

"It is, sir, but there's been a development that we need to bring to your attention."

Bruce O'Hara just stood there glaring for a moment. Finally, he opened the door fully, allowed them to enter. Having closed the door behind them, he led them into the living room.

"Is there anyone else here, sir?" Sands said.

O'Hara shook his head. "What is it?" he said impatiently.

"We've had some trouble with the...uh...woman whom we discussed."

76

"Exactly what does that mean?" O'Hara said as he reached for the cigarette box on his coffee table.

"It's her lawyer, Barbara Harris," Beadle said. "She's hardballing."

O'Hara lit a cigarette. "I was told that you would be responsible for anything further," he said. "That you people would handle this sort of thing."

"At that point we thought we had everything under control," Beadle said. "Barbara Harris is the one who's thrown a monkey wrench in the works. She wants more money for her client."

Bruce O'Hara ran a hand through his hair. Deliberately, he sat down on the sofa. "You people are cops. Can't you just...do something to scare her?"

"This lady shyster has been around Las Vegas for a long time. The bitch knows how to count. If she's not taken care of, she won't hand *us* up...just *you*."

O'Hara snuffed out the cigarette in the ashtray. "Shit. Goddammit."

"She's pushing for a hundred thousand," Ray Beadle said.

"Out of the question," O'Hara said. "Totally out of the question. I won't pay it."

"As I was saying, that's what she is *pushing* for. But I think we can get her to settle for less...a lot less."

O'Hara stood up, paced across the room.

"The captain and I figure that if we take her fifty and tell her that's all she's gonna get, she'll take it and that will be that," Sands said. "But if we don't do something you can be damn sure she'll make a move."

"My bet is that the sorry-assed bitch will peddle the story to the *National Enquirer*," Beadle said. "That's why we feel it's better to have her inside the tent pissing out rather than outside the tent pissing in. So to speak."

"What's to stop her from making demands on me again?" O'Hara said after a while.

"That's not her style," Beadle said. "I've known the sorry-assed shyster for many a moon. She's reasonable.

77

She'll settle for a piece of the pie. I personally guarantee it."

"What I'm finding out here is that personal guarantees don't mean shit."

"We're trying to do the best for all concerned, Mr. O'Hara," Sands said. "It's just that human behavior is unpredictable."

Bruce O'Hara reached for the cigarette box, snatched another smoke. He lit up again, walked to the window, and looked out at his well-manicured lawn. "What happens if I just tell this lawyer to go straight to hell?"

"We take a chance of losing control of the situation. But it might work...all or nothing."

"I really have no choice, do I?" O'Hara said. Sands noticed the crack in his voice.

"It's entirely your decision, sir," Sands said in his best in-command tone. "And I want you to know that if you decide to refuse to pay her and let the story come out, the captain and I intend to return the money you provided us. We'll return every dime."

Sands and Beadle drove O'Hara to the bank, where he withdrew fifty thousand dollars in hundred-dollar bills, then dropped him back at his residence. With the bag of money on the seat between them, Sands steered out the circular driveway and down the street. "That one about pissing out of the tent was great," he said.

Beadle grinned proudly, leaned back in the seat, and laughed.

Along with the rest of the passengers on the flight from Los Angeles, Sands and Beadle waited anxiously at the baggage area. Finally, the suitcase in which Sands had put the fifty thousand dollars made its way onto the conveyor belt. Sands breathed a sigh of relief. He reached down, picked it up, carried it outside.

Sitting in his car in the parking lot, Sands counted out fifteen thousand dollars for the grinning Beadle, who, as he was handed each stack of bills, thumbed them like a bank teller.

"I never thought it could be that easy," Beadle said.

"It's a great life, partner."

After dropping Beadle off at the Plush Pony, Sands drove to an exclusive jewelry store at the Hilton Hotel and purchased a gold necklace for cash. On his way to Monica's apartment, he was careful to maintain the posted speed limit, mindful of the money he was carrying in the trunk. He parked the car in the carport and hurried upstairs with the suitcase. Monica was sitting in front of the television. She was wearing a shortie nightgown.

"Hi, babe," she said.

He opened the suitcase, poured the cash onto the floor in front of her. She stared at the money for a moment, then came to her feet and embraced him.

Sands picked up the phone, dialed a number.

"Who are you calling?"

"Big Bruce," he said to Monica. "You do the blow-off." He handed her the receiver, moved to an extension phone, picked up the receiver as O'Hara answered.

"Mr. O'Hara. This is Barbara Harris of Harris and Goldfarb. You needn't say anything over the phone, sir. I'm calling to let you know that I have received the item you sent and that my client and I are fully satisfied. You will hear nothing of the matter ever again." As she spoke, Sands fastened the gold necklace around her neck.

"Uh...thank you. Thank God this thing could be worked out," O'Hara said.

Monica took Sands's hand, thanked him with her eyes.

"Thank you, Mr. O'Hara," she said. "I'm pleased that the matter was resolved discreetly. Goodbye, sir."

"Yes. Goodbye. And thanks again."

The phone clicked. Sands and Monica set their receivers down quietly. He moved to her. Reaching behind her, he slipped his hands under her panties, pulled her to him. "Thirty-five thousand buckaroos, lady."

They kissed passionately. "I love the necklace."

"What should we buy, hon?" he whispered as their lips parted.

"What I want only costs thirty-five dollars."

"Name it."

"A marriage license," she said.

Their eyes met, and for a moment Monica's face held the precise expression he had imagined during the interminable days and nights he had spent in his prison cell, the totally feminine, submissive, nurturing, loving, trancelike look that had been designed by the forces of nature to bring men to women.

"Let's get married right now," he found himself saying.

"Do you mean that?"

"I've never meant anything more in my life. I love you."

She hugged him desperately. "I don't ever want to be away from you," she said.

12 Sands drove to City Hall to get a marriage license, then to the Plush Pony to pick up Beadle, the best man. They drove down the Strip to the Church of the Heather Wedding Chapel, a tiny building with a tiny steeple, located in a corner of the gigantic parking lot surrounding the Sands Hotel and Casino.

Inside, standing before a miniature altar which faced empty miniature pews, a tuxedoed hillbilly with a greasy pompadour and liquor on his breath administered brief vows. Sands and Monica kissed.

Outside, Ray Beadle popped the cork on a bottle of champagne he had brought with him, and the three drank from the bottle on the way back to the Plush Pony. There Beadle dragged them to the crowded bar and ordered drinks for the house. He introduced them to the bar regulars, including some ex-cops who remembered Sands. As the night wore on, and as Tex, the purple-lipped cocktail waitress, brought endless rounds of drinks and bottles of champagne to their table, Eddie Sands felt he was back in the real world, for the first time since he'd been released from Terminal Island.

It was six-thirty in the morning.

Novak pulled the G-car to the curb in front of Haynes's home. Haynes shuffled out the front door with a steaming cup of coffee in each hand. Novak unlocked the door from the inside, shoved it open. Haynes handed a cup of coffee to Novak, climbed in. Novak pulled away from the curb.

In a few minutes they were out of the residential area and headed out of town.

Novak sipped his coffee, felt its warmth spread to his insides.

Red Haynes blew on his coffee. "With Bruno dead, we're no closer to making a case on Parisi than we were a year ago," he said.

Novak nodded. "You're right."

"And after what happened to him we'll probably never be able to convince anyone to testify against Parisi."

"We'll find someone," Novak said.

Haynes muttered something, blew on his coffee a couple of times, took a sip.

Novak steered onto open highway. The trip to Los Angeles took about four and a half hours. A mile or so south of the Los Angeles Coliseum, Novak steered onto an offramp to Central Avenue, a wide street extending through the Watts area, L.A.'s black ghetto. They cruised slowly along the avenue past run-down pool halls, shine parlors, liquor stores, storefront churches, and boarded-up establishments of all kinds. As they passed groups of people lingering on the sidewalks, they sensed hostile looks.

Haynes pointed across the street to a car lot with six

or seven passenger cars on it, most of them several years old. "There it is," he said. The faded wooden sign read "Mel's Used Cars and Rental Service." There was a small house trailer in the middle of the lot.

Novak made a U-turn and pulled to the curb in front of the place. They climbed out of the G-car, approached the trailer. The door was open. Inside, sitting at a card table reading a newspaper, was a bald, bespectacled black man who looked to be about Novak's age. He wore a faded black suit, white shirt, and bow tie. They stepped inside the trailer. The black man set the newspaper down.

Novak reached into his suit jacket for his badge.

"You don't have to show me no badge," the man said.

"Is this Mel's Rental Service?"

The man nodded. "That's right. And I be Mel."

Novak stepped to the card table, showed a card on which he had noted the license number of the car he had seen leaving the Stardust parking lot. "We'd like to find out who rented the car that bears this license plate," he said as the man eyed the card.

"Like to help you out, but all the leasing records done burned up in a fire."

Haynes and Novak looked at each other.

"So you don't know who you've leased cars to?" Haynes said.

"Not until all the records get restored."

"When will that be?"

"Might take years. Fire is a terrible thing."

Novak glanced about the office. There was not a scrap of furniture in the room.

"How long have you been out?" Novak said.

"Outta what?"

"Out of the joint."

"How can you tell I done been in the joint?"

"Same way you could tell we're cops, I guess."

Novak turned, walked out of the trailer. Haynes followed. They moved toward the G-car.

"You gonna just walk away?" Haynes said.

83

"Yes."

"I say we go back in there and turn that monkey upside down."

Novak unlocked the driver's door. "He's just a body paid to sit by the phone. They wouldn't leave him there if he knew anything."

They climbed in the G-car. Novak started the engine.

"A license number used to be a good clue," Haynes said.

"Time's are changing."

"For the worse."

The trip to Terminal Island Federal Prison took less than a half hour, straight down the freeway to its end. There, in the prison administration building, Novak and Haynes went through the usual routine of showing identification, signing various logs and forms. Finally, a young khaki-uniformed prison guard showed them down a well-waxed hallway to a door marked "Assistant Warden." He opened the door. A man with short, thick arms and a fireplug torso stood up from a cluttered desk and introduced himself as Ralph Dandridge. Novak noticed that the collar on his short-sleeved white shirt was frayed.

Dandridge offered seats.

Novak sat down in a chair in front of a barred window. Below, on a diamond which was part of the prison recreational yard, men dressed in blue denim played softball. "We're looking for someone who we believe may have been released from here recently," he said. "We're trying to put a name with a face."

"What else can you tell me?"

"I know what the guy looks like. He might be a confidence type. That's about it."

"When do you think he was released?"

"Within the last couple of weeks. Just a guess."

Dandridge nodded. He turned, grabbed a thick three-ringed notebook from a shelf behind his desk. He handed it to Novak. "This has a mug shot and identifiers on every inmate released during the last three months."

Novak turned pages. In the center of each page was a photo of a sad-looking man. Page after page of sociopaths, deviates, freaks, killers, all of whom, dressed in anything other than prison denim, would be indistinguishable in a crowd. After turning fifty pages or so, Novak found the man he had seen leaving Tony Parisi's room at the Stardust. The name printed on the top of the page was Sands, Edward L. "This is the guy," he said.

Dandridge left his seat, came around the desk to see. "Eddie Sands," he said. "Las Vegas police detective. Or was. He was released on parole August twenty-ninth."

"What can you tell me about him?" Novak said.

"When he first came in we put him in protective custody because he was an ex-cop," Dandridge said. He moved to a metal filing cabinet and pulled open a drawer. "But he asked to be let out on the yard right away. I couldn't believe it." He pulled out a file, carried it back to his desk, and sat down.

"What happened?" Novak said.

"Strangely enough, there were no problems," Dandridge said, opening the file folder. "Even though he was an ex-copper, nobody on the yard so much as gave him a dirty look."

Red Haynes cracked his bony knuckles. "You saying the man had some horsepower behind him?"

Dandridge nodded. He leaned back in his chair. "Instead of making him eat dick, the other prisoners kept out of his way right from the beginning. They showed respect like they do to the heavies. This was right from the get-go."

"Did he hang around with anyone in particular?" Haynes said.

"The man was a loner. Or at least he was while he was in here. But when he needed something he went to the guineas—the Mafia assholes. I've got quite a few of 'em here. This Sands had access. In fact, they even assigned him a slave."

"A slave?" Novak said.

"A gofer. Somebody to carry messages, run errands for him. That kind of shit. His name is Lopez, Pepper Lopez. He's a doper."

"We'd like to talk to him," Novak said.

"Lopez was released on parole a couple of days before Sands. He served five years."

"Who visited Sands while he was in here?" Novak said.

Dandridge flipped pages in the file again. He stopped. "A woman named Monica Brown visited him almost every other week...and he received a lot of letters from her." He picked up a pen and wrote on a note pad. He tore off the sheet and handed it to Novak. It read: "Monica Brown. 37654 Tropicana Lane, Las Vegas."

"What's Sands been up to?" Dandridge said.

"Believe it or not, that's what we're trying to figure out," Novak said.

Dandridge closed the file folder. "Nothing would surprise me. His parole release came earlier than it should have. It looked like a fix. Don't quote me on that."

13 Novak and Haynes stopped at Utro's Café in San Pedro for a quick lunch of hamburgers and beer, then headed north on the Harbor Freeway. Because Novak had once been stationed at the FBI's Los Angeles field office, he found his way easily to the San Diego Freeway and then the Santa Monica Freeway.

A half hour or so later, Novak steered off onto Santa Monica Boulevard, a street that was an odd mixture of old office buildings, yuppie establishments—health-food, sporting-goods, and frozen-yogurt stores—and faddish restaurants that he knew were mostly second-rate and overpriced. A block or two west of the freeway he pulled into the parking lot of a convenience store. Inside, he purchased a box of confectioner's sugar. At a pharmacy across the street he purchased, from a skeptical pharmacist, a small empty glass vial. He jogged across the busy boulevard back to the G-car and got in behind the wheel. He opened the box of sugar and filled the vial with the white substance, then snapped the plastic cap on the vial and shoved it into his jacket pocket. He tossed the box of sugar into a trash can a few feet away.

"What was that all about?" Haynes said.

"Insurance papers."

"No one could ever accuse you of not being prepared," Haynes said.

Novak started the engine, headed west toward the ocean. He could smell the salt air, and at the end of the busy street he could see the opening to the Santa Monica Pier.

Where the boulevard ended at the ocean, Novak turned left and steered along a section of commercialized coastline burdened with liquor stores, ten-seater bars, and plateaus of apartment houses which, like monuments to generations of greedy builders, effectively blocked one another's ocean view. South of the Santa Monica Pier, Novak drove down an incline leading to the beachfront. He parked.

Novak and Haynes climbed out of the sedan and made their way along a trash-strewn bicycle path past a building which Novak remembered from his time in L.A. as a halfway house for drug addicts. The beach itself was crowded with bathers of all ages.

A hundred yards or so down the strand, Novak spotted a pair of young policemen sitting at a table in front of a small fast-food stand facing the water. The young officers, one white and the other oriental, were dressed in the beach-beat uniform of short pants, tennis shoes, T-shirts, and baseball caps bearing police emblems. Novak showed his badge. "We're looking for a hype named Pepper Lopez," Novak said.

"We know him," the oriental cop said. He hoisted a small bag of french fries and poured some into his mouth. He pointed in the direction of the run-down fast-food and souvenir shops near the pier. Sandwiched among the dying establishments was a bar with a flaking wooden sign above its door. The Mermaid. The cop swallowed. "He hangs out there with all the other dopers. What's he wanted for?"

"We just want to talk to him," Novak said.

"Have you ever met him?"

Novak shook his head.

"He's been around. If you want something from him, you'll need a hook."

"Any suggestions?"

"He's always arrestable," the other cop said. He pointed to his forearm. "Tracks."

"What's it like in there?" Haynes said.

"A toilet. Ex-cons, hypes, muscle freaks. If you're going to take him out, you'll need backup."

The beach cops finished their last few bites of lunch as they followed Novak and Haynes along the strand to the Mermaid. Novak stepped through the front door into the semidark and was hit with an odor combining beer-soaked wooden flooring, marijuana smoke, and armpits. The cops aimed flashlights at an eighteen-seater bar filled with men and women who looked as if they just stepped off a prison bus.

Lopez was sitting near the rear door.

"Don't shine that light in my face, pig," said a drunken woman with a beehive hairdo. She wore a halter top and had a large tattoo of what looked like a spider on her left shoulder.

Cautiously, Novak moved down the bar toward Pepper Lopez. Haynes followed. The police officers beamed the flashlights here and there. As Novak reached Lopez, he flipped out his badge. "Let's go outside and talk, Pepper," Novak said.

"What for?"

"Let's go outside."

"You don't have to go nowhere, Pep," said a bearded, long-haired man sitting near him.

"He didn't do *nawwtheeng*," said a Mexican man with a Fu Manchu mustache.

A muscle-bound black man stood up slowly from the

bar. Deliberately, he moved in front of Haynes. He leaned forward until they were nose to nose. "Why don't you mothafuckas get yo asses outta here and leave us the fuck alone?" he said.

Haynes punched him squarely on the nose. Others at the bar jumped up. The cops swung nightsticks. People fell down, shouted. Glass broke. Lopez pushed off the bar stool and ran for the back door, and Novak tackled him. He dragged Lopez to his feet, snapped handcuffs on his wrists.

Haynes backpedaled past him, connecting with rifle-like jabs as the black man, bleeding but game, stalked him in a wrestler's stance. "Come on, spook, you wanna fight?" he jeered. "C'mon, spook." The oriental cop swung his nightstick and struck the black man on top of his head. The black man dropped, unconscious.

Holding Lopez by the collar, Novak dragged him past the others and backed out the front door.

Outside, a police car squealed to a stop. Two officers with nightsticks hurried out and huddled quickly with the beach cops.

"Thanks," Novak said, and gave a wave. The beach cops waved back. Novak and Haynes moved away with Lopez as the cops, nightsticks at port arms, rushed back into the bar.

In the distance, there was the sound of a siren.

Red Haynes made his way slowly through the stop-and-go traffic of downtown Santa Monica. Novak sat in the backseat with Pepper Lopez, who had to lean forward because his hands were handcuffed behind his back. "What are you arresting me for?" Lopez said.

"You have tracks. That's a violation of your federal parole."

"You didn't even look at my arms before you arrested me."

As Lopez squirmed with his handcuffs, Novak leaned back in the seat. Outside, the sidewalks were crowded with the beach town's eclectic population, rich westsiders in khaki pants and designer polo shirts, college kids wearing overalls and other pseudo-farm gear, garishly dressed blacks, punk rockers, and the modestly attired elderly who all seemed to be walking dogs.

"Actually, we're interested in someone you did time with."

"I ain't no fucking stool pigeon, man."

Two hours later, in a carpeted interview room in the Los Angeles Strike Force office, Novak sat across a small table from Pepper Lopez, who, probably because he needed a fix, was squirming in his seat. Haynes leaned against the wall.

"Why are you so worried about answering a few questions about Eddie Sands?" Novak asked, for probably the fiftieth time.

"Fuck all this, man. If you're gonna put me back in jail, why don't you just go ahead and do it?"

"I'll tell you why," Novak said. "Because I feel bad about locking up a man who just got out. It's not something I want to do. You can ask my partner here. He'll tell you that if there's one thing in the world I hate to do, it's lock up a man who's just hit daylight."

Pepper Lopez started to rub his scarred forearm. He stopped himself and wiped his wet palms on his trousers. He formed a wry smile. "My parole officer can't bust me just for having marks. This ain't like the old days."

Novak took out the sugar-filled glass vial and palmed it. He moved close to Lopez, reached into Lopez's shirt pocket, and feigned finding the vial. He held it up for Lopez to see. "But he will for possession."

Lopez clutched his shirt pocket, came to his feet. "There wasn't nothing in my pocket! You put that there!"

Novak handed the vial to Haynes. "Tag this and list it on an evidence receipt, Red. We'll turn it over to Federal Parole."

"You salted me!" Lopez said with his hand still

clutching his shirt pocket. "I'm gonna tell my parole officer you salted me!"

Novak shrugged. He sat down at the table. "He won't believe you. All hypes lie."

14 Lopez's eyes blinked rapidly as Haynes opened a folder, tugged out a narcotics evidence form, and began printing Lopez's name on the top line.

"This ain't right, man," he whined.

Novak stared at Lopez as Haynes continued with the form. "Sit down," he said.

Lopez continued to stand. "You people are playing head games with me."

Suddenly Novak sprang across the table and with both hands grabbed Lopez by the collar, yanked his face close. "No, it proves that we aren't playing games," he hissed. "It means that unless you start talking, your ass is headed back down to Terminal Island."

"I don't know nothing about him."

"We heard that you were his right-hand man in the joint," Haynes said.

Novak shoved Lopez away.

"I got a habit, man," Lopez said. "In the joint I did things for the people who kept me supplied."

"That's understandable," Novak said in a calm voice.

"When Sands first came in, some people asked me to take care of him...to make sure he was protected."

"*Which* people asked you?" Novak said. He sat down again.

"Some people who are connected."

"Tony Parisi's people?"

"I ain't naming no names."

Red Haynes interlocked his fingers. With a sharp outward motion, he cracked his knuckles. Lopez turned to see what the sound was.

"What kind of guy is Sands?" Novak said.

"He's not like most cops."

"How do you mean?"

"He can talk, man," Lopez said. "He can talk real smooth like a lawyer. Better than a lawyer. And he's always thinking ahead. Like if that happens then this will happen. That kind of shit. That's how he ended up in the joint. He was fixing cases for the big boys in Las Vegas. He was a detective."

"Did he tell you what he was gonna do when he got out?" Haynes asked.

"He said he was going to be a private eye and make a lot of money."

"Who is Monica Brown?" Novak said.

"His main squeeze. He had her picture up in his cell."

"May I ask you a question?" Novak said.

Pepper Lopez formed his eyes into slits.

"Is there *anything* you can give us on Sands? Because if there isn't, we're all wasting our time. I mean, like if you really don't know anything about the man, we've got the wrong guy, and you're going back to the slammer."

Lopez's eyes opened. "That's what I been telling you all along. I don't know nothing about the motherfucker."

94

Novak and Haynes exchanged shrugs. Slowly, Haynes lumbered off his chair. He reached behind his back and unsnapped handcuffs from the keeper on his belt. He motioned for Lopez to stand.

"What happens now?"

"We take you to your parole officer."

"He'll send me back to the joint for sure."

"Talk to us, Pepper."

Lopez sighed deeply. "There was talk he was going to get early release because his people were paying off somebody at the Federal Parole Board," Lopez said after a while. "There was talk about it on the yard."

Novak stared at Pepper Lopez for a moment. "And that's all you know about him?"

"I swear on the name of my mother."

After another half hour or so which netted them no further information, Novak and Haynes led Lopez to the front door of the office and allowed him to leave.

On the way back from Los Angeles, Novak and Haynes stopped in Barstow, a sweltering desert town of service stations and coffee shops, which existed for no other reason than that it was halfway between L.A. and Las Vegas. Having filled the tank at a crowded service station, Novak steered the G-car into the parking lot of a coffee shop that looked reasonably clean.

Inside, a beefy waitress wearing a starched, sweat-ringed beige uniform that was a size too small set menus and glasses of water on their table.

"How much bribe money do you think it would take to get somebody out of the federal joint?" Novak said.

"A lot. The guys on the Federal Parole Board aren't gonna risk their asses for a dollar and a quarter. And a bag man had to be paid. There's always a bag man. Probably some rotten, greedy lawyer."

The waitress returned to the table with a coffeepot. Haynes covered his empty cup. "I hate coffee." She drew the pot back, filled Novak's cup. They ordered hamburgers.

"If you were the king hood in Las Vegas, what would make you go to the trouble of getting someone out of jail?" Novak ruminated.

"Money."

"Where is an ex-cop gonna come up with a load of money?" Novak said as he stared out the window at a tour bus that was unloading elderly passengers returning from Las Vegas.

"Maybe he's gonna work it off."

"Could be."

After finishing the hamburgers, Novak and Haynes got back on the road. Haynes took the wheel. They drove about twenty miles without speaking.

"How did you ever find your way into the Bureau?" Haynes said.

"I was in Army Intelligence. When I got back from Nam the Bureau was hiring."

"What did you do in Army Intelligence?"

"Interrogated prisoners of war, wrote reports." Novak lit a cigarette, dropped the match into the ashtray.

"Torture 'em for information?"

"Some guys did. But it doesn't go very well. People get pissed off when you torture them."

"Ever ask yourself why?" Haynes said. "Like why did you become an FBI agent instead of delivering mail or selling insurance?"

"We're in it because we get a charge out of it," Novak said. "We get a charge out of catching the bad guys."

"Why didn't you ever remarry?"

"I almost did, was even engaged," Novak said. "I was stationed in Mississippi. She was a schoolteacher."

"What happened?"

"A civil-rights case. I interviewed a female prisoner in the local jail. She tells me the sheriff has been raping her in her cell. I get a written statement, the U.S. attorney files a case on the sheriff. The sheriff counters by accusing me of raping the woman I interviewed while I was in her cell and gets the local district attorney to file a complaint against me. Instead of backing me up, the Bureau transfers me. To New York."

"And your fiancée refused to make the trip?"

"She didn't want to leave her teaching job to live in New York," Novak said.

"I bet you thought about quitting the Bureau," Haynes said.

"The thought crossed my mind. But it's not really the Bureau that's to blame...just the people in it."

Red Haynes gave him a puzzled look.

The only sound for some time was the humming of wheels against scorching desert highway. His eyes on the white line in the road that seemed to stretch forever before him, Novak considered what he knew about the case.

"Somehow or another Parisi found out what we were up to with Bruno," he said finally.

"Maybe Bruno was killed for some other reason. Maybe he owed someone money. Maybe..."

"Parisi is cautious. He would never have authorized the hit if he didn't know for sure."

"Where do you think the leak is?" Haynes said as he upwrapped a stick of gum, offered the package to Novak. Novak declined.

"It could be a member of the federal grand jury. It could be a clerk in the mail room who happened to read one of our reports. Who the hell knows?"

"It might be Frank Tyde."

"Tyde is too lazy to be a crook."

Haynes thought about it. "Good point."

In the Strike Force office early the next morning, John Novak thumbed through a file drawer until he found a file on Eddie Sands. He removed the file from the drawer and took it to his desk. In it was a case report which recounted, in summary form, the details of Sands's indictment, arrest, and conviction. Witnesses had testified that while a member of the Las Vegas Police Organized Crime Intelligence Squad he was funneling information to Parisi concerning investigations directed against him.

Also in the file was a one-page Las Vegas police form,

entitled "Intelligence Contact Report," which read as follows:

CONTACT: Aug. 29
REPORTING OFFICER: Fisher, J. Serial #94429
DETAILS OF CONTACT WHILE ON ROUTINE TRAFFIC PATROL.

I stopped a vehicle bearing California license plate 547 MEM. The car was driven by Edward Sands, whom I knew as a former fellow Metro officer before his arrest and conviction. I issued a verbal traffic warning in lieu of citation. Sands said he was working as a private investigator. No further information. This contact report prepared because Sands is listed in Field Interview computer as an organized crime associate of Parisi, Anthony.

On a page titled "Personal History of Intelligence Subject," someone had filled in blanks to show date of birth, fingerprint classification, and other details. In the right-hand corner of the sheet was a section marked "Associates." There was only one name listed: Raymond K. Beadle.

Novak left his desk, searched through a card file in the corner of the room. There was only one card bearing Beadle's name. It was marked "Possible assoc. Sands, Edward, per CI #98634.

In a numbered file which was kept in the office safe, he recovered an informant card on Confidential Informant #98634. It was a woman named Florence Bradshaw. The last entry on the card had been made by Frank Tyde. It read: "Negative Contact with CI"—a federal-law-enforcement euphemism which meant that Tyde had not taken the trouble either to contact the informant or to remove her name from the active files. He copied the woman's address on a three-by-five card, shoved the card in his pocket.

Later, Novak wandered down the hall and found

Frank Tyde standing in front of the sink in the tiny coffee room holding a foot-high plastic statuette of an immodest cherub boy under a running faucet. "Remember an informant named Florence Bradshaw?" Novak said.

Tyde finished filling the statuette with water. "Watch this," he said as he set the statuette on the counter. He pressed a button and the plastic cherub boy pissed a curved stream of water into the sink. "It's for my bar at home. The wife loves these."

"Florence Bradshaw. Does the name ring a bell?"

"Florence Bradshaw... Florence Bradshaw," he said. "A cocktail waitress at the Plush Pony?"

"That's the one."

"She was a witness." Tyde pressed the button a second time. He grinned proudly as the cherub boy functioned again.

"To what?"

"There was some muscle work that took place outside the Plush Pony. She was there but refused to sign a statement." He pressed the button on the statuette again. There was another stream of water. "Some guy got his leg broken by some collectors for a bookie. He owed three grand or something, so the collectors waited until he left the bar. One guy held his arms and the other one whacked his right leg with a Louisville Slugger. She saw everything. Elliot wanted me to handle it as an organized-crime case, but I kissed it off. Just because somebody gets their leg broken doesn't mean it's organized crime." He turned the statuette upside down, emptied the water into the sink.

"How about the name Ray Beadle?"

"I think that was the name of the guy who was supposed to have swung the bat. An ex-cop."

"What did she say about him?"

"She claimed she couldn't identify anybody because she was drunk. Even the victim wouldn't give a statement. The whole thing was a bag of worms. I kissed it off." He set the statuette in a box. "I can't decide whether to fill this thing with scotch or bourbon."

Later, Elliot came into the squad room to arrange red thumbtacks on an outdated Organized Crime graph he had pinned to the bulletin board.

"Someone coming from D.C.?" Novak said as he lifted his suit jacket from the coat rack.

"Head of OC Section from Justice will be in tomorrow morning. The quarterly inspection."

Novak nodded, shrugged on his jacket.

"Briefings for the brass bore you, right?" Elliot said.

Novak shrugged. "I guess you could say that."

"This is a mistake," Elliot said. "Because in reality there is nothing else. I realized it as soon as I was sworn in as a U.S. attorney."

"I don't think I follow you."

"This is a job, a way to earn a living. And graphs, boards, bullshitting the people from D.C., this is what it's all about. You can make big cases, convict a hundred organized-crime figures, but no one really cares. The way to get promoted is by show and tell."

"I guess that's one way to look at it."

"When D.C. has a promotion to hand out, they don't check arrest statistics. They're looking for someone who can *present* himself, make a good show at Congressional budget hearings. Someone who *looks the part*. Sure, I'm interested in making cases, but looking the part is where it's at. Am I boring you?"

Novak smiled, shrugged.

"You've got a lot of leadership ability, Novak. If you'd play the game you could get promoted, become an agent-in-charge somewhere."

"I'll think about it," Novak said, though the idea disgusted him. In fact, Elliot disgusted him.

"During the inspection I'm going to be asked about the Bruno Santoro murder. What's the status?"

"Red and I are working on it, but as of right now there's nothing," Novak said.

Elliot stabbed another tack into the board. "We need to solve this one. Parisi meant this as a message. If we can't solve it, other witnesses will never come forward against him. He knows that."

"It'd be nice to know how Parisi found out about Bruno," Novak said.

"My guess is Parisi was using Bruno until things got too hot," Elliot said. "Parisi gives Bruno some info on one of his competitors, Bruno tells us. We were arresting people Parisi wanted to be arrested. How's that for a scenario?"

"If that was happening, Bruno would have realized it."

"I'm afraid I have little faith in informants," Elliot said.

Novak noticed that some of the names listed on the chart on the bulletin board were those of Las Vegas organized-crime figures who were dead. He wondered if the OC section chief would notice this when Elliot gave his quarterly enthusiastic briefing on the current Nevada organized-crime picture. He guessed not.

"Faith has nothing to do with it," Novak said. "It's just that I've been doing this for a long time and I think I would have been able to tell if an informant was taking me for a ride."

"I hope you don't take what I've said in any derogatory sense."

"I'll make the case," Novak said. "It might take a while, but I'll make the case."

"Love that spirit," Elliot said. "I'm behind you one hundred and fifty percent."

 **15** John Novak steered his G-car down a narrow street which was only a block or two from the casinos. It was lined with recently built two- and three-story apartment houses—the stucco prefab variety that, like the plethora of casinos that had sprung up around town in the past few years, were designed for speed of construction. Flaking stucco was everywhere and cracks at window joints were clearly visible.

Novak pulled to the curb and turned off the engine. He found the name Florence Bradshaw on a mailbox at the entrance to the place, climbed a flight of stairs, knocked on the door of Apartment 7. The door was opened by a barefooted woman wearing shorts and a soiled T-shirt which clearly showed her nipples. Her lipstick was purple and her head was wrapped in a dye-stained white towel.

"Florence Bradshaw?"

She nodded.

Novak showed his FBI badge and identification card. "May I come in?"

"Do you have a search warrant?"

"No. I just wanted to ask a couple of questions."

"Questions about what?"

"About what happened outside the Plush Pony the night the man had his leg broken."

"You can ask your questions right here at the door."

Novak glanced both ways in the hall. "I think it might be better if we could talk where we can't be overheard," he said in his best disarming manner. Florence Bradshaw stared at him for a moment. He gave her a little smile. Hesitantly, she stepped back and allowed him inside. He closed the door softly as she moved to a cluttered end table, grabbed a pack of cigarettes, and lit up. "You can sit down if you want," she said with a mouth full of cigarette smoke.

"Thanks," Novak said. He ambled to a cigarette-burned dinette table, discreetly avoiding a yellowed brassiere that was lying on the floor. He sat down. The table was a sea of wadded-up Kleenex surrounding a ceramic bowl filled with a dark liquid. Next to the bowl was an empty box of hair dye, a sheet of newspaper, a *Playgirl* magazine.

"I'm assigned to the Federal Organized Crime Strike Force. We investigate extortion committed to collect debts. It's against federal law."

"Well, you must have a hell of a lot of business in this town."

"May I call you Tex? The nickname was in the police report."

She came to the dinette table and flicked an ash into a plastic ashtray brimming with purple-lipsticked butts.

"Might as well," she said nervously. "That's what everybody else calls me." She pulled a chair back from the table, sat down.

"Tex, there's a chance that you might get called before

103

a federal grand jury to testify about who broke that man's leg."

"I got nothing to testify to because I didn't see a damn thing. I was drunk."

"You were working that night."

"That doesn't mean I wasn't drunk."

"Funny things happen around a bar all the time. I wouldn't blame anyone for not wanting to get involved. Particularly when it involves some heavies...leg breakers."

Tex removed the towel covering her wet hair. With cigarette dangling, she dipped the comb in the bowl, then ran the dripping implement through her hair. She tapped the comb on the newspaper. It made a line of black dots. "If somebody don't pay their gambling debts in this town and get theirselves in trouble it's none of my damn business." She set the cigarette in the ashtray, took a few more comb strokes.

"The U.S. attorney-in-charge of the Strike Force is making a big issue out of the case," Novak said. "He wants to make an example out of witnesses like yourself who refuse to make statements against leg breakers."

She stopped combing. "What do you mean, make an example?"

"He says that if people won't do their citizen's duty he'll swear them in in front of a federal grand jury anyway, and if they refuse to testify he'll throw them in jail for contempt." Novak reached into his suit jacket, took out a subpoena. "I'm sorry. This isn't my idea." He set the subpoena on some wadded Kleenex next to the bowl of dye.

Her eyes were on the subpoena. "There's people around the Plush Pony who'd kick my ass if they so much as heard I was within a mile of a federal grand jury. They would kick my ass till my nose bleeds. Or worse."

"Maybe the subpoena will make it easier for you. No one could blame you for testifying to keep yourself out of jail."

"Don't give me that thing. I'll leave this town before I'll testify."

"This is a federal investigation. If you left town a material-witness warrant would be issued for you. You'd be arrested and brought back."

Tex tossed the comb down on the newspaper. "I haven't done anything wrong," she said, her voice cracking. "Why should I have to testify?"

Novak sat there a moment as if he was making up his mind. Then he picked up the subpoena. "Could I trouble you for a cup of coffee?" he said.

"Coffee?"

"I could sure use a cup."

Tex left the sofa. She found a clean cup in the cupboard, spooned in instant coffee, added water, set the cup inside a microwave oven. She closed the oven door. The microwave hummed. She looked at him. He slipped the subpoena back into his suit jacket.

"I don't know the man who got his leg broke. He was in the bar and that's all I know," she said, facing the oven.

"I'm not interested in the victim, only in the leg breakers."

"The FBI man who interviewed me that night...Mr. Tyde? He wasn't very interested. He only stayed a few minutes."

"Do you know a man named Ray Beadle?"

"No."

The microwave oven stopped humming. She opened the oven door, took out the coffee, set it in front of him. He thanked her.

"He hangs out in the Plush Pony," Novak said.

"I'm a cocktail waitress. I may have served him. You take sugar?"

Novak shook his head. "Black's fine." He sipped the bitter coffee. "A lot of ex-cops hang out there, right?" he said.

"That's why I like working there. I don't have to worry about getting raped," she said, sitting down at the dinette table. "And if I wanna make it with someone I don't have to worry about getting AIDS." She picked up her comb, dipped it.

"If you could help me clear up a few things, maybe it wouldn't be necessary for you to testify. Whatever you tell me would be just between the two of us."

"I don't know."

"I'm trying to give you some slack. If I wasn't, I could just serve the subpoena on you and let nature take its course."

"Ray Beadle is a real honest-to-Christ gentleman. He and I had a few drinks one night and ended up here at two in the morning. Rather than trying to put the make on me, he just had a drink and left. I thought that was damn nice. It's not often I get treated like a lady."

"Have you heard the name Eddie Sands?"

"I may have."

"What's he into?"

With her hair hanging dark and wet, Tex reached for her cigarette. It had gone out. She relit the butt, blew smoke. "I don't have no idea what he's into. Eddie... well, I guess you know he just got out?"

"Right."

"He could have taken Ray down with him when he got arrested. Ray told me that."

"On what?"

"They were into some shakedowns and stuff when they were on the police department. They would take a guy's money and then let him go."

Tex picked up the bowl, carried it, moved across the room to the kitchen counter. She poured the hair dye over the dirty dishes piled in the sink.

"What else do you know about Eddie Sands?"

"He just got married to a woman named Monica Brown. She pulls confidence games. That's what I've heard."

"What variety?"

"Phony stock and investments, I think. Eddie's really in love with her. I can tell that kind of thing. God knows

106

I've been in love enough times myself." She took a big drag from her cigarette and smashed it into the ashtray.

"Thanks for taking the time to talk to me," Novak said as he stood up. He made his way to the door.

"That's all? I'm not gonna have to testify?"

"Tex, never say that a fed hasn't done you a favor."

 **16** It was Sunday.

Eddie Sands, whose body clock was still on prison time, woke up early and spent an hour or so reading the newspaper, sipping coffee, and munching cinnamon toast, things he had often dreamed of doing when he was in prison.

Monica, barefooted and wearing a loose-fitting robe, wandered through the living room into the kitchen. She picked up the coffeepot off the kitchen stove, poured a cup. She yawned. "I had a weird dream last night. I was floating across Las Vegas in a hot-air balloon and people were shooting at me with rifles, trying to kill me. The bullets were coming through the floor of this wicker-basket thing under the balloon, so I was hiding in a corner of the basket." She blew on the coffee.

"What finally happened?" he said, after a while.

"I was pressing so hard against the side I could feel the wicker biting into my face. The bullets kept popping through the floor closer and closer to me...ping, ping, ping. All of a sudden, the side of the basket breaks open and I go tumbling out. As I was falling through the air I was trying to scream, but I had no voice." She sipped coffee.

A telephone rang. Sands picked up the receiver.

"Is this Edward Sands?"

"Who's calling?"

"Special Agent Novak, FBI. I'd like to get together with you for a few minutes today."

"What about?" Sands said after a pause.

"I'd prefer to talk in person. Can you meet me in my office at the federal courthouse...say in an hour?"

Another long pause.

"I guess so," Sands said.

"I'll give your name to the guard at the back door." The phone clicked. Sands eased the receiver down to the cradle. "The FBI wants to talk to me."

"Oh, no. Oh, God."

He left the table, moved across the living room to the window. "If they were going to arrest me they wouldn't have called. They would have come here."

"This is Sunday," she said. "They wouldn't be working on a Sunday if it wasn't something important." She came to him. "What if it's Bruce O'Hara? What if he went to them?"

"The feds like to play head games. They like to fuck you around. There is nothing to worry about," he said, though he knew there was.

He showered, shaved, and dressed carefully, taking his time because he didn't want to let the feds think he had hurried to meet them. But on the other hand, he didn't waste a *lot* of time. He certainly knew it wasn't a good idea to piss off a cop.

As he drove into the rear parking lot of the modern Las Vegas Federal Courthouse, Sands checked his wristwatch. It had been slightly over an hour since he'd received the phone call. He parked his car in the near-empty lot and made his way to the rear door of the building. A uniformed building guard unlocked the door from the inside. Sands gave his name. The guard, a sleepy-eyed black man, led him to the fourth floor. The guard knocked on a door marked "Organized Crime Strike Force," then withdrew. Almost immediately, Novak opened the door. He introduced himself courteously, without offering his hand, then led Sands into an interview room off the reception area. He closed the door behind them.

"I hope I didn't alarm you," Novak said, as they both took seats at the table, which had nothing on it except an ashtray.

"What's up?"

"Your name came up during the course of an investigation," Novak said offhandedly. He shrugged off his suit jacket, hung it neatly on the back of a chair. "Kinda hot in here. Care to take off your coat?"

Sands, who was becoming irritated, shook his head no.

"You were just released from Terminal Island."

"That's right. And I used to be a Metro detective, and I just got out of the joint, and it's Sunday, and you called me down here to ask me some questions. So go with the questions."

Novak nodded politely. "I checked your file," he said. "You were convicted of doing some favors you shouldn't have done for Tony Parisi—for giving him inside information on police investigations, fixing cases for people who worked for him. He must have trusted you."

"That was before I got caught."

Calmly, Novak folded his hands. "What are your plans now that you're out?"

"Haven't made any plans."

"Have you seen Tony Parisi since you were released?"

"I've seen a lot of people since I got out. I don't keep a list."

110

"Tony's done real well in the past couple of years. He's used his muscle in the right places. In fact, you could say he's got a lock on the town. The casinos are bending over for him. In Las Vegas he's the man to see."

Eddie Sands drummed his fingers absentmindedly, then thought better of giving away the fact that he was nervous. He stopped.

"Having been a Metro detective," Novak continued, "you know how it is when somebody gets big in town. The analysts in D.C. write up an organized-crime profile. Then they lean on the Strike Force to do something about it. They want results."

"What exactly are we talking about?"

"Pardon me?"

"Am I being investigated?"

"No, just Tony Parisi."

"Then what say we cut the smokescreen bullshit and get to the point?" Sands said.

"I apologize for taking your time on a Sunday," Novak said. "The reason I called you down here was to give you an opportunity to assist in the Parisi investigation. We're looking for someone who can help us put the picture together on Parisi."

"Okay, you're looking for a super-snitch who can do Tony Parisi. Well, I don't know anything about Parisi, and even if I did, I would rather eat a hundred miles of shit than rat on someone. See, nobody likes a stool pigeon. Not cops, not crooks. Nobody in the whole wide world, including you, has any respect for a goddam rat."

"I'm talking about paying a sizable reward for each piece of information, plus expenses. Putting you on the federal payroll," Novak said.

"You must think you're talking to some clown you picked up off the street."

"No, I think I'm talking to a guy with a lot of street sense. That's one thing cops like you and me have that no one else in the world can buy—street sense. We know how the game is played."

"Being an informant is too far for me to go, Novak.

That's the name of that motherfucking tune."

Novak took a government ballpoint pen from his shirt pocket. He set it on the table, spun it like a propeller. "Somebody will."

"Huh?"

"What I'm saying is that *somebody* will go that far. Somebody who has a problem and wants it solved, somebody who wants to make a lot of government reward money. Somebody who Tony stepped on, maybe a competitor, will come out of the woodwork and set Tony up."

Eddie Sands cleared his throat. He feigned being attentive, the way crooks used to with him when he was on the police department.

"It happened to Al Capone," Novak continued. "It happened to Joey Gallo. And it'll happen to Tony Parisi. One of Tony's friends will turn, and Tony will go to the joint."

Eddie Sands gave a scornful laugh. "So what? Do I give a shit about Tony Parisi? Go ahead and lock him up."

"Before Tony is locked up, there'll be a big grand-jury investigation. People will be named. A lot of them will go to prison. The question is, on which side of the witness stand would you rather be?"

"When I was a cop I used to give that same little lecture to bullshit people into becoming informants," Sands said. "I had a lot of luck with it." He considered laughing as he made his point, thought better of it, and just smiled instead.

"How did you treat those who wouldn't cooperate?" Novak said. His expression was icy.

There was a long silence. They stared at each other, neither one flinching or blinking.

"I guess that means you're gonna try to squeeze me into being an informant," Sands said.

"Thanks for coming in," Novak said.

Sands rose, moved to the door. Novak kept his eyes on him all the way out of the room.

Outside in the courthouse parking lot, Red Haynes, having used a Slim Jim lock-picking device to gain entry, sat in the front seat of Sands's car. He examined the miscellanea in the glove compartment, carefully piling the items on the seat next to him in the same order as he had removed them, all the while keeping his eye on the door of the building that faced the parking lot.

When he found something important, he noted it on a pad which he kept in his shirt pocket. So far, the list read:

1. One receipt for a necklace costing $3467.57 from David and David, a jewelry store located in the Hilton Hotel on the Strip.

2. One map of Beverly Hills, bearing a penciled circle on Rexford Drive.

3. Car-rental papers reflecting that Sands had rented the car in Los Angeles under his own name.

4. One credit-card sales receipt reflecting a purchase of gasoline at a service station in Beverly Hills.

He was just about through when the building guard exited the door of the courthouse, looked in his direction, and putting two fingers to his lips, gave a whistle, then hurried back inside.

**17** Haynes shoved the items back in the glove compartment, stepped out of the car, and closed the door carefully. As he moved quickly across the parking lot and around the side of the building, he saw the guard open the door. Eddie Sands stepped out and headed toward his car.

At the front door of the courthouse, which faced Fremont Boulevard, Red Haynes let himself in with a key.

Novak was waiting in the lobby. "Come up with anything?"

Haynes pulled out his pad. "Not a hell of a lot. He rented the car a week before he was released. Filled the tank in Beverly Hills once. Has a Beverly Hills map with a mark on Rexford Drive. He bought a thirty-five-hundred-dollar necklace two days ago at the Hilton."

Novak nodded.

Haynes shoved the notebook back in his shirt pocket. "What did he have to say?"

Novak moved to the glass door facing the street. He watched as Eddie Sands drove out of the parking lot and entered the stream of traffic on the busy boulevard. "He says he doesn't want to play informant. He's a stand-up guy."

"Now what?"

John Novak was in a trance. "Parisi helped Sands get out of the pen," he said. "Parisi mentions the name Bruce O'Hara in front of Bruno. Sands gases up his car in Beverly Hills, while he's on prison work release."

"Dope. It must have something to do with dope," Haynes said. "Bruce O'Hara is probably a dope addict, like everybody else in Hollywood. A nose-packer. Who the hell knows?"

Novak shrugged, continued to stare at nothing in particular. "So let's ask him."

The next day, in the desert about a hundred miles east of Los Angeles, Novak made a left turn off the interstate highway and, following the directions given him over the phone by Bruce O'Hara's Hollywood secretary, continued along a dirt road leading toward the base of a small mountain range. Haynes pointed to a solitary, weather-beaten single-story dwelling far in the distance, amid sagebrush and cacti.

"That's the kind of place I'd like to live in when I retire," Haynes said.

"There's nothing out here."

"That's the point. No neighbors. No relatives. No crooks. No Elliot. Just peace and quiet twenty-four hours a day."

"You'd go crazy."

"I already am crazy."

Novak said nothing.

"Can you imagine this bearded wimp who's never worked a day in his life getting paid to sit behind a desk and tell people to run if they feel stress?"

To Novak's right, near some large sand dunes, was a formation of film trucks and other studio vehicles. Novak maneuvered the G-car over to the trucks. He stopped in front of a middle-aged uniformed studio cop who was rubbing a piece of ice across his sunburned forehead. Novak showed his badge. "FBI. We're here to see Mr. O'Hara." Without replying, the studio cop turned and marched toward a sand dune where a group of camera and sound technicians were arranged around three men costumed in the kepis and short-sleeved khaki uniforms of the French Foreign Legion. He waited as a man with a clapper moved in front of the camera. The studio cop said something to one of the men. The man turned in the direction of the G-car.

"That's him," Red Haynes said.

Bruce O'Hara stared at them for a moment, then, followed by the studio cop, approached. The agents climbed out of the G-car.

O'Hara led them into a carpeted and well-furnished mobile dressing room. Having offered them chairs, he tossed his kepi on a dressing table, lit a cigarette, paced a bit. "What brings the descendants of J. Edgar Hoover out here to this miserable suffering desert?" he said in a way that made Novak suspect he was worried about something rather than just curious.

"During the course of an investigation it was reported to us that a man named Anthony Parisi had mentioned your name," Novak said. "Do you know him?"

"Are you talking about the Parisi who's been in the newspapers recently? The Las Vegas mobster?"

"Yes."

"Do you know him?" Haynes said.

O'Hara gave him a condescending look. "As a matter of fact I don't. What did he say about me?"

"He said your name a few times while speaking on the phone."

O'Hara smiled wryly. "And you were eavesdropping on him, right?"

"Actually an informant told us he heard him."

O'Hara took a puff on his cigarette, blew a thick smoke ring. "What did he say about me? Don't I have a right to know that?"

"He just mentioned your name," Novak said, watching the smoke ring.

"I was recently in Las Vegas. We were shooting some scenes near Boulder Dam."

"But if you've never met the man, there probably would be no reason for him to be concerned with you shooting some scenes at Boulder Dam," Haynes said.

O'Hara pulled a director's chair away from the wall and moved it closer to them. He sat down. "Who is this informant you're talking about? Or is that some big state secret?"

"Bruno Santoro," Novak said.

"This whole matter sounds a bit bizarre."

"He was blown to bits. A car bomb," Haynes said.

Bruce O'Hara furrowed his brow. "Am I in any danger?"

Novak shrugged. "All we know is that Tony Parisi brought you up during the course of a conversation."

Haynes cracked his knuckles. Bruce O'Hara cringed. "This is all very strange. I really don't know what to tell you," he said as if to close the conversation.

Novak reached into his jacket pocket and removed a mug shot of Eddie Sands. He offered it to O'Hara. O'Hara took it to the dressing table. He removed a pair of French-frame eyeglasses from a leather case, put them on, examined the photograph. He swallowed, visibly lost color in his face, and sat down in his chair again. He handed the mug shot back to Novak. "Who is he?" he said, clearing his throat.

"Eddie Sands, an ex-con and ex-cop...one of Parisi's associates," Novak said.

"Ever seen him before?" Haynes said.

O'Hara removed his eyeglasses. "Can't say as I have." He returned the glasses to their case.

"Can you think of *any* possible reason why Parisi would mention your name?" Novak said.

O'Hara fidgeted in his seat, checked his wristwatch. Novak noticed that it was a gold Rolex. The thought passed through his mind that a real Foreign Legionnaire would never be able to afford such an expensive wristwatch.

O'Hara left his seat again, moved to the window. The movie star stared out at the desert for a moment. "No, I can't," he said finally.

"Have you ever had any business dealings with the Stardust Hotel and Casino?" Haynes said.

Without averting his gaze from the window, O'Hara shook his head.

"Have you been the victim of a crime recently?" Novak said.

"No," O'Hara said without hesitation. He turned and moved to the dresser. He slapped on his kepi. Eying a mirror near the door, he adjusted the brim. "I'm sorry I can't help you, gentlemen," he said. The agents stood up and moved toward the door.

"If there's anything you'd like to tell us, I promise it'll go no further," Novak said.

"Sorry I can't help you, gentlemen," he repeated, making it clear that the meeting was ended. He reached for the door handle, opened the door.

"Mr. O'Hara?"

O'Hara turned.

"Do you still live in Beverly Hills?"

O'Hara nodded. "Yes, 11379 Rexford Drive."

Novak handed a business card to O'Hara. "If you remember anything, I'd appreciate a call," he said.

"He looked like he was going to faint dead away when you showed him the mug shot," Haynes said as they climbed into the government sedan.

"We hit a nerve all right," Novak said. "We definitely hit a nerve."

"I bet it has something to do with dope. Dope is ruining the world. It *has* ruined the world."

"Eddie Sands has never been involved with narcotics," Novak said as they climbed into the sedan. "He went to prison for muscling people who owed Parisi money...fixing cases for the mob." Novak started the engine. "That look on O'Hara's face meant that something is *wrong*," he said as he steered toward the highway.

"We'll probably never find out what it is," Haynes said. "The bug on Parisi didn't do any good. No one in Vegas will say a word about him, including Eddie Sands. The bag job on his car was a waste of time. You didn't even get anything out of that waitress. We're spinning our wheels."

The wind was blowing as Novak left the dirt road and returned to the highway. Large tumbleweeds crossed in front of the car, and he could feel the wind trying to move the vehicle into the oncoming lane.

"Not really," Novak said. "We found out that Eddie Sands just got married."

As Haynes turned to him with a puzzled look on his face, Novak pressed the accelerator closer to the floor.

 **18** It was eight in the evening by the time Novak and Haynes arrived back in Las Vegas. Starving, they stopped at a fast-food place near the MGM Grand and picked up hamburgers and coffee. At the federal courthouse, Novak steered the G-car into a parking place. They went inside.

In the Strike Force office, Novak shrugged off his suit jacket and draped it on the back of his desk chair. Haynes tore open the food bag and spread it out on his desk. He tossed a burger to Novak. Novak took a big bite of the burger, then opened the top drawer of his desk and removed a manila file folder labeled "Brown, Monica S."

A sound came from the hallway. The door opened. Frank Tyde stepped into the room. "What were you guys doing over in L.A.?" he said.

"Nothing much," Novak said, flipping through the file. Ignoring Tyde, Haynes ripped open a ketchup packet and emptied it on his burger.

"Big day here. I spent the day filling out an expense voucher," Tyde said as Haynes took a big bite. "Then I got a shoe shine, bought some pencils at the government store, made a few phone calls."

"Why are you still here?" Haynes said with his mouth full.

"A guy from the New York office told me he'd try to get back to me today on a records check." He checked his wristwatch. "I'm waiting for him to call back."

Haynes swallowed, sipped his coffee. "It's eleven P.M. in New York," he said. "The office is closed."

Tyde folded up a newspaper that was spread out on his desk. He shrugged. "I know. But the three hours overtime I picked up waiting for the call maxes me out on overtime for the month."

Novak continued to flip pages in Monica Brown's file. He stopped at a recent citizen-complaint report from the Salt Lake City FBI office. It read as follows:

> On August 12, one Mabel Kincaid (F, W, 63 yrs) was interviewed at the Salt Lake City Office at her request. She stated substantially as follows: On or about July 4–7 she visited Las Vegas, Nevada, to attend a quilting convention. While there she met Subject who told her she was an investment counselor specializing in investments for persons of retirement age, and described a trust involving the assets of a gold mine which was to be secretly sold by a member of a wealthy family and which would provide dollar-for-dollar profit for investors who were able to take advantage of this inside information.
>
> After Kincaid returned to Salt Lake City, she received a telephone call from Subject. Subject pitched her again with the investment and emphasized that if she didn't act quickly the chance for a quick profit would be lost. After repeated

telephone calls from Subject Kincaid finally sent a total of $3,000 by means of a U.S. Postal Money Order to Monica Butler, Las Vegas, P.O. Box 5657. After Kincaid forwarded the money she never heard from Subject again. A check with the U.S. Postal Inspection Service, Las Vegas, revealed that P.O. Box 5657 was rented under the alias Monica Taylor. The driver's license used by the woman who rented the box (same general description as Subject) was determined to be bogus.

FOLLOW-UP INVESTIGATION

Bureau records show names Monica Butler and Monica Taylor as aliases used by one Subject, whose true name is Monica Brown (FBI #591360087). Subject was investigated by the San Francisco field office for similar scam three years ago. San Francisco case was declined by the U.S. attorney due to lack of prosecutive merit in that Subject, though she had been investigated for numerous confidence games, had no prior conviction for a similar offense.

CASE DISPOSITION

Because victim has no witnesses to the alleged scam, U.S. attorney Salt Lake City has declined to prosecute Subject.

Because U.S. attorney has declined to prosecute, no further investigation will be conducted. Info provided to Las Vegas for whatever disposition you deem appropriate.

Frank Tyde shuffled to the front door. "See you tomorrow, guys."

Neither man replied. Tyde opened the door and left.

"I'm looking through Monica Brown's package again," Novak said.

"I read it," Haynes said as he continued to eat. "Sounds like Salt Lake City kissed off a good case."

"I think we should try to revive the issue."

"How so?"

"Victims of confidence games never tell the full truth the first time they are interviewed."

"Gimme the game plan."

"I think you should head for Salt Lake. Reinterview the victim. In the meantime, I'll stay here and set up on Monica Brown."

"We're going to focus in on the *girlfriend* of a guy who we see meet *once* with Parisi?" Haynes said. "Aren't we getting a little off base?"

"I don't think so," Novak said.

It was as hot as Las Vegas could get.

Heat rose from the asphalt in the parking lot of the Silver Dollar Motel, blinding sun ricocheted from the chrome and glass, and the air was hellishly dry. Monica pulled into a parking space which she knew Leo could see from his room and climbed out of her Porsche. Carrying a large, heavy straw purse, she ambled past the registration office to the pool. She sat down in a deck chair and kept an eye on Leo's room.

Leo peeked from the blinds, disappeared. The door to his room opened and he shuffled out, wearing his uniform of Hawaiian shirt and soiled white trousers. As he headed in her direction, he looked about suspiciously in an attempt, she thought, to show what a cool operator he was.

"I figured you'd be back," Leo said. He pulled up a deck chair, noted what appeared to be melted and dried ice cream stuck to its seat, shoved it away, and grabbed another. He sat down.

"I don't really give a shit what you figured," Monica said.

Leo looked at the dirty pool. "You *are* here for chips?"

"How many have you got?"

"Two hundred grand worth."

"I'll take them all at twenty points."

"That will cost you forty K."

"I'm ready."

Leo removed a package of cigarettes from his sagging shirt pocket, tapped out a cigarette. He removed a silver cigarette holder from a trouser pocket, blew into it, inserted the cigarette.

"Did you hear what I said?" Monica said.

He flamed the cigarette, sucked smoke. "Sounds like you have a backer."

"That's right."

"I don't want to meet anyone."

"You don't have to," she said.

"Your money man is going to trust you with the entire transaction?" Leo said as smoke wafted from his mouth. He waved his cigarette holder through it.

"You show me the phony chips, I show you my buy money. We make the exchange, just like that."

Leo shook his head slowly.

"Why are you shaking your head?"

"You show me your buy money. *Then* I show you the chips and we do the deal."

"Okay."

Leo seemed taken aback. "Just like that?"

"I'm ready to deal. I didn't come here to sit by this scummy pool."

Leo looked around carefully. "I guess we should make arrangements to see your buy money."

"Once I show you the forty thousand, I don't intend to sit on my ass and wait to get ripped off."

Leo smiled. "You won't have to. Everything can be done in a matter of minutes. The chips are nearby."

"So, for instance, if I was to show you forty grand right this very minute, when could you deliver?"

Leo's expression turned serious. "Within five minutes."

Immediately, Monica lifted the flap on her purse, showed him it was full of banded bills. She closed the flap. "I have a gun. If you're thinking about ripping me off, you'll have to kill me right here in public." She looked at her wristwatch. "You have five minutes."

Leo stared at her for a moment. Slowly, he stood up, looked about carefully. There was no movement in the parking lot. Suddenly a nearby door opened. Two swim-suited young black boys rushed out of a pool-front room yelling. They ran to the pool, jumped in, and began splashing about.

Leo turned, moved deliberately toward his room. At the door, he stopped, noted that Monica was still sitting by the pool. He unlocked the door, entered the air-conditioned room. Cautiously, he moved to the window, looked out again. He told himself that Monica was too confident, moving too fast...but he had seen the money. Nervously, he checked his watch. "Fuck it," he said out loud. He hurried to a door leading to an adjoining room, unlocked it. Inside the other room, which a friend had rented for him, he flicked the air-conditioning control to the off position. He stepped up onto the bed, removed the grate from the overhead air-conditioning duct, and dropped it onto the bed. Carefully, he reached inside the ceiling space and, one by one, took out four heavy packets of counterfeit gaming chips. He set them on the bed, refixed the grate. Quickly, he gathered up the packets of chips and made his way back into his room. He dropped the packets into a plastic laundry bag. Carrying the bag, he moved to the front door and opened it.

Standing in front of the door were two men dressed in business suits. The younger man flashed a badge. "Nevada State Gaming Commission," he said. The older, crew-cutted man standing next to him slammed a fist into his chest and knocked him violently backward into the room. He dropped the gaming chips as both men lunged for him. His face was shoved against a wall and he felt fingers searching his waistband, legs, and torso. His right arm was twisted behind his back. Handcuffs were snapped on his wrists. He was shoved into a chair with such force that it hurt his tailbone. He felt flushed, nauseated.

Eddie Sands leaned down, picked up the plastic laundry bag. He opened the bag and looked inside, dumped the contents of the bag onto the bed. Using a penknife, he slit open one of the packets. Gaming chips fell out. Sands picked up one of the chips, held it up to the light of the window. He made eye contract with Leo. "What's your name?" he said.

Leo swallowed twice, and looked up at Ray Beadle. "Can I have a cigarette?"

Beadle socked him squarely on the nose, flipping him backward off the chair and onto the carpet.

"Leo Gordon. My name is Leo Gordon."

Sands moved to the bed, sat down. He looked at Leo.

"Where are the rest of the chips?" he said.

Leo didn't answer.

Beadle moved to the dresser. He picked up a Coca-Cola bottle, lobbed it directly at Leo. The bottle made a bonk as it struck him squarely on the forehead. Leo yelped and cringed.

"My partner asked you for the rest of the chips," Beadle said.

"There aren't any more!" Leo said.

"Where did you have them hidden?" Beadle demanded.

Leo's terror-filled eyes turned toward the door leading to the adjoining room. Beadle grabbed him by the hair and shoved him into the room. Leo nodded toward the air-conditioning duct. "In there," he said.

Beadle stepped onto the bed, ripped the grate away from the ceiling. The duct was empty.

"And now the cash," Sands said.

"The cash?"

"That's right, asshole, the *cash*," Beadle said as he stepped off the bed. "The money you've made peddling chips."

Leo didn't move. Sands reached into Leo's rear trouser pocket, pulled out his wallet. Inside were three hundred-dollar bills. He pulled them out, tossed the wallet onto the bed. "Is this all?"

"Do I get a receipt for that?"

Beadle punched Leo in the stomach. Leo dropped to his knees, gagged, tried to catch his breath.

Sands shoved the bills into his pocket. "Don't make us tear this room apart."

"That's all the money I have," Leo sputtered. "So help me." His eyes were watering from the blow.

"Mr. Gordon, you're under arrest for the felony crime

of possession of counterfeit gaming chips," Sands said as he reached into his shirt pocket, took out a small card. He read: "Before we ask you any questions you must understand your rights. You have the right to remain silent. Anything you say can be used against you in a court or other proceedings. You have a right to a lawyer. If you do decide to answer you can stop the questioning at any time to consult with a lawyer. If you cannot afford a lawyer and want one, one will be appointed for you at no cost. Do you understand those rights?"

Leo Gordon nodded his head. "Yes."

"Are you willing to answer some questions?"

A tiny rivulet of blood had crept from Leo's right nostril to the edge of his upper lip. "I'm not sure I—"

"Before we book you," Sands interrupted, "there's a couple more things I want you to understand. First of all, our job at the Gaming Commission is not simply to arrest dealers, middlemen like you. Because gambling is the major source of revenue for the State of Nevada, our goal is to determine where and how counterfeit chips are made . . . and to put the makers out of business. To do that, the Attorney General has authorized us to deal for information. I mean deal right here and now. Do you understand what I am telling you?"

Leo licked blood off his lips. "You want me to be an informer."

"You might say we're offering you the opportunity to cooperate and assist the State of Nevada."

"That bitch Monica is working for you, isn't she?" Leo said. "She set me up."

He cringed as Ray Beadle stepped close to him. "We ask the questions, clown," Beadle said.

Sands eyed the telephone on the dresser, nodded to Beadle. "Call for booking approval," he said. He turned back to Leo. "Of course she's working for us. We have a forgery case on her, and she decided to do herself a favor and cooperate. The lady has smarts. She saw the light."

Leo blew air through his bloody nose a few times. Sands pulled him to his feet, ushered him to a chair near the window. "How long can I get for this?" he said.

Beadle picked up the phone receiver. He dialed.

"Five years," Sands said. "Ten if you have a previous record. In Nevada there's no slap-on-the-wrist-and-probation for chip-counterfeiting cases. The judges here are all ex—casino mouthpieces. They'll knock your dick in the dirt."

Leo moved his gaze from Sands to Beadle, then back.

"Lemme speak to the on-call deputy DA," Beadle said in a tone of voice that Sands thought was a little too histrionic.

"What happens to me if I tell you what I know?" Leo said.

Sands leaned against the wall. "That depends on what you tell us."

"What if, say, I knew where the chips are coming from ... who's making them?"

"Then I call my boss for approval and we make a deal."

"This is Agent Trout," Beadle said to the receiver. "Gaming Commission. We've just arrested a male adult with a load of those Stardust chips that have been going around. I'd like approval to book and a bond recommendation."

Leo looked at Beadle, then back to Sands.

"Yesterday Monica was sitting in handcuffs like you are right now," Sands said. "A big forgery jacket hanging over her head. Now her case will be dismissed. The State of Nevada helps those who see the light."

Leo made a contorted attempt to wipe some of the blood from his upper lip onto his shirt. He missed, looked at Sands as if to ask for help. Sands stared coldly at him.

"Does a deal mean I won't have to spend any time in jail?" he said.

19 Sands sat in the backseat of the sedan with Leo Gordon. As Beadle drove slowly down Tropicana Boulevard past the Convention Center, Sands gazed out the window with a bored cop-escorting-another-asshole-to-jail expression on his face.

Beadle, his collar soaked with nervous perspiration, was driving. Sands wished he would stop glancing in the rearview mirror every three seconds as if he were driving a truckload of dynamite.

"Why will I have no chance to post bail?" Leo said.

"Because you're not a U.S. citizen. If the judge granted bail you might run back to Liverpool or wherever the fuck you're from."

"I've never been in an American jail."

"Should be real interesting cross-cultural experience," Sands said.

"Particularly if you enjoy being fucked in the ass by red-blooded American Negroes," Beadle said. "They'll be drawing straws for your hips."

"Very funny."

Beadle had slowed to about thirty miles per hour. He made a turn on Fremont. The jail was less than a block away. He turned in the seat and made eye contact with Sands. Sands blinked twice to reassure him.

Beadle drove directly into the jail parking lot, pulled into an empty parking space, turned off the engine.

Two uniformed policemen walked past them on their way to a radio car.

Sands hoped that Leo wasn't looking at the rearview mirror, because Beadle's face had a confused, tortured expression.

"Last chance to play *Let's Make a Deal*," Sands said as Leo stared straight ahead at the imposing modern jail building. He could hear the other man's breathing.

"I scored the chips in the Bahamas ... in Nassau," Leo said.

Eddie Sands felt a sense of relief which, he admitted to himself, approached actual sensual pleasure.

"From who in the Bahamas?" Sands said.

"From the bartender at the Colony Inn. I placed an order for the chips. This chap delivered to me three days later. I paid two percent."

"Got a name?" Beadle said. He was now fully soaked with perspiration.

"Uh ... the bartender's name was Cyril. I never knew his last name."

Beadle looked about nervously. He took out a handkerchief, wiped his face and neck.

"Where are the rest of the counterfeit chips?" Sands said.

"That's all I had. I swear to God."

"And the cash? The money you made from dealing? Where is it?"

"You said if I agreed to cooperate I would be released."

"Part of cooperating is turning over the fruits of the

crime. To make a clean breast of things."

"Are you going to keep my money?"

"The money will be booked as evidence and you'll be given a receipt. When I have your case dismissed you'll receive the cash back. Of course, the state keeps the phony chips."

Leo Gordon, clammy-pale, cleared his throat. "The rest of the money is at the airport," he said.

Beadle started the engine.

At the Las Vegas Airport parking lot, Sands removed Leo's handcuffs. Inside the terminal, Leo led them to a rental locker. He handed Sands a key. Sands opened the locker. Inside was a leather briefcase. Sands snapped open the latches. He counted the small bills it contained. "Seven thousand two hundred dollars," he said. Sands reached into his inside jacket pocket, removed a small printed form—"Evidence Receipt"—which had the logo of the Las Vegas Metropolitan Police Department in its upper-right corner. Beadle handed Sands a pen. Sands filled in the amount on the form, separated the carbon copy from the original. He handed the receipt to Leo.

"Now what?" Leo said, shoving the receipt in his pocket.

"Now you set up a buy of chips from Cyril the bartender," Sands said. "When he delivers we arrest him."

"So that means we are going to Nassau."

"No shit, Kemo Sabe," Beadle said.

Sands checked his wristwatch. "Do you have a credit card?"

Leo nodded.

"Buy a ticket to Nassau. We'll meet you there tomorrow after we book the evidence and get the deal formally worked out with the district attorney."

"How will I find—"

"Name a hotel," Sands said.

"The...uh...the Crown Retreat."

"We will meet you in Nassau at the registration desk of the Crown Retreat Hotel at five p.m. tomorrow,"

Sands said. "If you're not there when we arrive, we'll have a warrant issued for your arrest. It will be waiting if you ever try to travel to the United States again or cross an international border." He checked his wristwatch as if considering a deadline he had to meet.

Beadle took the briefcase. Leo stared at it for a moment, then at Sands and Beadle. He turned and headed toward the ticketing area. After he was out of sight, Sands and Beadle hurried out of the terminal. Outside, they shook hands and broke into a fit of laughter so uproarious that tears streamed from their eyes.

"What would you have done if he hadn't caved in at the jail parking lot?" Beadle managed to say between fits of laughter.

"How the hell do I know?" Sands said.

"I wonder how long he'll wait at the hotel?"

For a moment, standing among hundreds of passengers hurrying in and out of the terminal, they just looked at each other. Then they broke into laughter again.

A young brunette secretary with thin, clear skin showed Bruce O'Hara into Mickey Greene's office. As usual, the gray-haired and goateed Mickey was on the phone. He shook hands with O'Hara and, keeping the phone to his ear, motioned him to a chair in front of his enormous cluttered desk. As O'Hara sat down, Micky Greene motioned apologetically with his hand.

As he sat there waiting for Mickey Greene to get off the phone, O'Hara surveyed the room with its futuristic plastic and glass furniture. The walls were covered with framed photographs—Mickey on his boat, Mickey and his dumb former Miss Universe wife, Mickey standing in front of his collection of restored antique cars, Mickey with things he owned. At that moment, it occurred to O'Hara that although he had visited the office many times before over the period of twenty years he had known Mickey Greene, he had never seen a law book. Not one. Even in the clutter on Mickey Greene's desk there was none to be seen. There were piles of thick entertainment contracts, but not one book. That was Mickey—a telephone to his ear, winging it, getting paid to push people to the limit. If there was a cartoon caricature of him, thought O'Hara, it would portray Mickey Greene with an oversized goatee and phone, sitting beside the pool at the Beverly Hills Hotel.

"You say you've learned a lot about the entertainment business?" Mickey Greene shouted into the phone, finally getting a word in. "Well, tell me this! *Did you learn not to fuck yourself?* That's the first lesson! Never bend your tool backward and *fuck yourself!* Because that's what you'll be doing if you don't sign the contract! Gotta run. See you at the Springs." He tossed the receiver back onto the cradle.

"Talk to me, Bruce. Tell me you've finished your crapola Foreign Legion movie. The screenplay made me throw up. You shoulda never done it. Dreck written by a shmeckler."

"I have a problem," Bruce O'Hara said softly.

Mickey Greene stroked his goatee. His face became somber. He moved a few feet to a cabinet, took out a bottle. Efficiently, he poured drinks, handed one to O'Hara, touched the intercom button on his desk. "Stop all calls!"

He sat down on the sofa and nodded to O'Hara.

"It finally happened," O'Hara said suddenly, finding that his throat was dry. He sipped the drink, almost coughed. "Someone found out about...uh...the...the things I do."

"You mean about the broads."

O'Hara looked at him.

"I want you to tell me everything," Mickey Greene said. "Leave nothing out."

"A few days ago this Las Vegas cop comes to my house. I mean, at the time, I thought he was a cop." O'Hara sipped more scotch and, in soft and quiet tones, related the entire story of the blackmail. By the time he was finished, Mickey Greene had refilled his glass three times.

"How do you know his name is Eddie Sands?"

"The FBI agents that came to the movie set showed

me a photo. They asked if I knew him," Bruce O'Hara said angrily.

"What did you say?"

"Nothing. I played dumb."

"At least you did one thing right."

"I didn't come here for a goddam lecture."

Mickey Greene plucked the glass from O'Hara's hand. He sauntered slowly to the liquor cabinet. He refilled their glasses and, using his hand, though tongs were available, dropped cubes of ice into the drinks.

"So that's about it," O'Hara said. He felt stupid, angry, embarrassed.

Mickey Greene handed O'Hara a full drink. "I'm sure you realize something has to be done. We have to move on this thing."

O'Hara left his chair, followed Mickey Greene across the room to a bay window which looked down on the sprawling Beverly Hills Country Club.

"You're Mr. America," Mickey Greene said. "You're wearing John Wayne's hat. If this trash comes out in the *National Enquirer* you won't be able to get a job as a fifty-dollar-a-day extra."

"I need your help, Mickey. You and I have known each other for more than twenty years. We've made millions of dollars together. I want you to handle this for me."

Standing in the light of the window, Mickey Greene, who had one of the deepest Palm Springs suntans in Hollywood, looked Mephistophelian. It's the goatee, thought O'Hara.

"Have you mentioned this to anyone else in the world?" Mickey Greene said.

"No."

"Have you even *hinted* to anyone else in the world about this problem?" Mickey Greene maintained eye contact as he spoke.

"No. You're the only one I can talk to. You know that."

"There's no going back once I set things in motion," Mickey Greene said after a while.

"Is there any possible way it could ever come back to

me? I want to know if there is even the remotest possibility that anything could ever come back."

Mickey Greene shook his head. "No. These matters are handled by people who will never know of you or me. Even the one man I deal with, whom I have known for as long as I have known you, won't know the reason for the request."

"How much will it cost?" O'Hara said.

"A lot less than you've already shelled out. I'll make all the arrangements."

"This Sands. He screwed me out of a hundred grand. Humiliated me."

Mickey Greene hoisted his glass to O'Hara's. "It's over now," Greene said.

The glasses clinked.

20 It was four in the afternoon on Roanoke Street, an East Las Vegas thoroughfare lined with stuccoed apartment houses that looked as if they had all been constructed from the same set of plans.

Sitting behind the wheel of a G-car parked across the street and more than half a block away from the entrance to the apartment where Monica Brown and Eddie Sands resided, John Novak half-listened to an all-news station. There had been a small fire in the kitchen at the Thunderbird...the Teamsters Union was threatening a strike at the Dunes...the chairman of the board of the Sahara had announced plans to expand the golf course. He'd been there since dawn, and he was fed up with news, talk, and music, any and all varieties. He was also weary of thinking about ways to trap Parisi, of reliving

Bruno Santoro's murder, and just of killing time. Monica Brown hadn't left her apartment all day.

He turned the radio off, rubbed his eyes, admitted to himself that the day had been wasted.

Suddenly the electric wrought-iron gate to the ground-floor parking area began to open. A silver Porsche cruised out onto the street and headed in his direction. It was Monica. He ducked down in the seat. The vehicle swished past. Quickly, he started the engine, made a U-turn. Monica made a left turn at the corner. He followed her at a discreet distance as she made her way to downtown Las Vegas. Having cruised along Fremont past the motels at the west end of Glitter Gulch, she turned right. As Novak made the right turn she was nowhere to be seen. He stepped on the gas, but had to stop at the next light. "Damn," he said out loud.

Believing he had lost her, he made a U-turn and drove into the parking lot of the shopping mall. He cruised along the rows of cars for a few minutes.

He finally spotted the Porsche parked in front of a small shop with a sign in the window which read:

MAIL SERVICES
Postal Boxes/Western Union

He parked a few cars away, climbed out of the G-car, wandered toward the shop. Through the bay window he could see Monica standing in front of a counter conversing with a cadaverous man wearing a tank-top shirt.

Novak walked into the place and stood in line behind Monica. The man took some envelopes from under the counter, handed them to Monica. Novak glanced over her shoulder as she checked the letters. All the envelopes appeared to have the same address:

Monica Butler, President
United Equity Mining Trust

She shoved the letters in a straw purse she was carrying, turned, and headed toward the door.

"Can I help you?" said the cadaverous man.

"Nice-looking lady," Novak said as Monica left.

"Gets lots of letters. What can I do you for?"

"Uh...how much is it to open a postal box?"

"Thirty a month."

"Little too steep for me," Novak said as he watched Monica climb into her Porsche. "Thanks anyway."

"You ain't gonna get a postal box no cheaper in this town," the man said as Novak moved away. As he stepped outside, Monica backed the Porsche out of the parking place and headed for the street. Novak ran to his car.

He caught up with Monica at the stoplight at Fremont and followed her directly back to her apartment. He returned to the spot where he had been parked all day. He made a note of the trip in his investigative log.

Soon it was dark and he found himself turning the radio on again.

The flight to Salt Lake City from Las Vegas was uneventful. Red Haynes located the government Chevy in the airport parking space where the Salt Lake City liaison agent had told him it would be. It took him no time at all to drive to Mabel Kincaid's suburban address: a one-story wood-frame house with a front porch that looked recently scrubbed.

He knocked on the door, heard footsteps. The door was opened by a hefty older woman, wearing a flower-print dress. Her white hair was wrapped tightly in a bun. Haynes showed his badge. "Agent Haynes, FBI. Are you Mabel Kincaid?"

"Yes, sir."

"I'm here about the fraud report you filed."

"Please come in."

Haynes followed her into a modest but immaculate living room. The furniture was sturdy and well-made, but old-fashioned. What looked like handmade quilts covered the sofa and walls.

"When I made the report I never thought anything would come of it. I'll never get my money back."

"There aren't enough agents to investigate all the cases that come in," Haynes said. "We're bogged down in paperwork and a rotten court system."

Mabel Kincaid made eye contact with Haynes. Her eyes were a penetrating blue. "It's noon. I'll bet you're hungry," she said.

"Not really," Haynes said, though he was starving.

"I grew up with six brothers and I can tell when a man is hungry," she said. She pointed him to a chair at the dining table, which was covered with a crocheted tablecloth. "You sit right down, Mr. Haynes," she said on her way out of the room.

Though Haynes protested, Mabel Kincaid brought food to the table, roast beef, salad, mashed potatoes—hell, he thought, maybe everything she had in the house. They ate and talked.

"I was at a convention in Las Vegas and this nice young woman, Monica Butler, struck up a conversation with me. She said she'd been raised in Salt Lake and that her father was an Elder in the church...just like my daddy. We had so much in common," Mabel Kincaid said as she kept an eye on his plate.

"A big line of bull...baloney," Haynes said. He finished off his mashed potatoes.

Mabel Kincaid immediately jumped up, grabbed the bowl of mashed potatoes, and, completely ignoring his protestations, ladled another heaping portion onto his plate. She sat down again.

"She called me when I returned home. At first we just talked. Then she suggested I invest the money from Daddy's estate—there wasn't much, about three thousand dollars—in the Gold Mining Trust. She said she'd actually been down in the mine and seen the vein of gold."

Red Haynes forked the last piece of roast beef on his plate, thought better of it, cut the piece in half, then ate it slowly.

"Looks like you can use a little more roast beef," she said.

Haynes held up his hands. "Can't eat what I have. Uh...what happened when you finally sent her the investment money?"

"That was the last I ever heard of her," Mabel Kincaid said as she forked a thick slice of roast beef, slapped it on his plate. "I tried to call, but she'd changed her number. It never occurred to me until that very moment that she was anything but an upright Christian woman. Right now I feel like the dumbest old turkey that's ever come along the pike." Using her cloth napkin, she wiped away a tear.

"Are there any witnesses to the conversations you had with her? To the times she made representations to you about investing in the trust?"

Mabel Kincaid shook her head sadly. Then a look of kindness came across her face. "I bet you could go for a nice slice of hot apple pie."

"Thank you, but there's no way I can eat anything else, ma'am. I mean that."

Mabel Kincaid carried the empty plates into the kitchen and returned with an enormous slab of apple pie. She stood over him.

Haynes shook his head. "No. Please. I've never eaten so much."

"There's something important I haven't told you, Mr. Haynes."

Haynes looked at her, then at the pie. She set it in front of him, then walked over to a china cabinet and pulled open a drawer. She removed a small cassette tape, handed it to him.

"What's this?"

"Before I sent her the money, I recorded some of her calls. Right here on tape are all the promises she made to me about that darn old Gold Mining Trust."

"Why didn't you give this to the agent you spoke with the first time?"

"Because I felt underhanded at having recorded the

calls without Monica's permission, and I thought there might be an outside chance that she would repent, someday, and give me back my daddy's money." She returned to her seat. "But something changed my mind."

Haynes shook his head.

"I was watching you sit here at the table where my daddy used to sit and I remembered something he once told us kids."

"What's that?"

"Destroy the seed of evil or it will grow up to be your ruin."

"I've heard that," Haynes said. And as Mabel Kincaid watched with pleasure, he took a healthy bite of apple pie and chewed slowly.

21 There was a metallic roar in the Stardust Casino, the sound of one-armed bandits eating money. For the life of him, Tony Parisi couldn't spot even one solitary slot machine that didn't have someone feeding it change. And the crap tables were hot. Plastic dice tumbled on green felt. Stick men changed numbers. Gaming chips were stacked, shuffled, collected.

Sitting alone at a cocktail table at the edge of the elevated portion of the casino bar, he surveyed the maelstrom of activity in the place. It was standing room only in the keno area, crowds at the busy blackjack tables, even a line waiting to get into the coffee shop. He knew that because of the table odds and the fix on the slot machines, every man and woman in the crowd, no matter how much or how little he or she chose to gamble, would eventually lose. He gazed down the enormous, high-ceilinged, plushly carpeted room full of losers, turkeys, cornball Okies, dumb farmers, cripples, tourists, and working stiffs from L.A. who were getting a charge out of pissing away their bucks. Fuck them and the station wagons and tourist buses they rode in on, he thought.

Mickey Greene, dressed in white trousers and a polo shirt, wandered into the bar area, spotted Tony Parisi. Parisi gave him a little wave. As Greene made his way to the table, Parisi took a sip of club soda, swished it around in his mouth, swallowed. They shook hands.

As Greene sat down, Parisi looked about the surrounding area for signs of the local cops, feds, or DA's investigators who he knew took turns surveilling him.

"Friends tell me things are nice for you here," Greene said.

A cocktail waitress dressed in a sarong came to the table. Mickey Greene ordered scotch and milk. She headed back toward the bar.

"Why'd you want to meet me in the bar?" Parisi said. "I don't like meeting people in public."

"Because when you're on vacation in Las Vegas you might just happen to see somebody in a bar and join them for a drink. If you go to a room, to the cops it means you *know* the person—it's a planned meeting. See, *I* think in courtroom terms."

"It's good to be careful."

The waitress returned with the scotch and milk, set it on the table. Greene dropped a ten-dollar chip on her tray. She thanked him, moved toward another table. Greene took a look around, lit a cigarette. "Are you in a position to have something done?"

Tony Parisi turned his palms up. "What are you talking about?"

"I'm talking about laying paper on somebody," Greene whispered.

"Who, why, what," Parisi said, as a statement rather than a question.

143

"I have a friend, and this friend is visited by a shakedown man...a phony-cop play. My friend shells out. This cocker is greedy, comes back, scores again. My friend wants off the hook. He wants the shakeman to disappear."

"The shakeman...is he connected?"

"Not that I know of."

"No problem as long as the man is not connected. But I can't get involved in a war."

"This is an independent operator...a shmeckler, a confidence man."

"Who are we talking about?"

"*Can* this be done?"

"As long as the guy is not protected by someone else's family, yes, it can be done, sure." Tony Parisi finished off his soda. He belched.

"How much?"

"The price is twenty-five large."

"Twenty-five? I was thinking more like ten."

"So I guess you wasn't thinking hard enough."

"Twenty-five is a lot of money."

"So do it yourself. Then it doesn't cost you shit."

"I never thought you would try to rip me off on something like this," Greene said. "I'm doing this for a friend."

"Is your friend broke? Maybe he lives in the poor section of Beverly Hills?"

"Be realistic."

"Poor people don't get shaken down," Tony Parisi said, staring at the waitress as she bent over a nearby table and showed cleavage.

"Let's call it fifteen," Mickey Greene said.

Parisi gave a little laugh. "Hire a junkie to do it for fifty bucks. Then he can point the finger at you on his way down the river."

Greene stared at him for a moment. He took out a pen and wrote something on a cocktail napkin. He handed the napkin to Parisi.

Parisi turned the napkin around and read: "Edward Sands—ex-cop in Vegas."

"Heard of him?" Greene said.

Tony Parisi shook his head slowly. "No," he said with a straight face. He checked his wristwatch, pushed his chair back, stood up, stretched, slapped his paunch.

"But can you find him?"

"For twenty-five I'll keep looking *until* I find him."

"What's next?" Greene said.

"I find this guy Sands, then I call you up. You bring me twenty-five. Then it gets done. That's all. What more do you want?"

It was ten at night by the time Novak discontinued his surveillance of Monica Brown's apartment. He was hungry, thirsty, and stiff from sitting in a car all day. He found himself driving toward Lorraine Traynor's home.

He arrived there a few minutes later, pulled into the driveway. The near-new two-story house was in one of Las Vegas's exclusive residential areas. Through the front window, he could see her sitting on the sofa next to a stack of thick books.

"Where have you been all day?" she said as she opened the door.

"Sitting on the place where Eddie Sands is living," he said, stepping inside. The living room was furnished with Victorian furniture, which Novak never found comfortable.

"The man you saw meeting with Parisi?"

He nodded.

"Learn anything?"

"His wife is running some kind of a scam."

"Doesn't sound like a very profitable day. Hungry?"

"Starving."

In the well-equipped kitchen, Novak stared outside at the pool as Lorraine pan-broiled a steak. He sipped a beer.

"I listened to the tapes of Parisi," she said. "I made some notes for you. There's nothing there. The tapes alone aren't enough to have him indicted for anything."

"He talks about people paying off."

"Nothing is definite. Not once does he make a definitive statement that could be used against him in court."

"Hoods don't make definitive statements about crimes they've committed."

She forked the steak out of the pan, set it on a plate, and put it in front of him.

"I can give you another eavesdropping order," she said.

He unscrewed the top of a bottle of steak sauce, poured it on the meat. "Parisi is too cagey on the phone. And he never uses the same room for longer than a day or so, which makes it almost impossible to plant a bug." He cut into the steak and ate.

"How about a search warrant?"

"Won't do any good."

"You sound as negative as Red Haynes," she said, sitting down at the table with him. She refilled his beer glass.

"Somehow or another I've got to get next to him."

"You sound like a crook talking."

"The game isn't all cut-and-dried like the case law you read," he said as he chewed. "Sometimes it gets real nasty."

"Taking cases personally isn't good for one's mental health," she said.

"Easy for a judge to say."

Nothing was said for a while.

"May I ask you a question?" Lorraine said.

"Shoot."

"Am I just a judge to you? Someone to bounce cases off of, someone to sign search warrants for you? Just an acquaintance?"

He stopped eating, looked into her eyes. "I didn't mean it like that, Lorraine. I'm sorry." Novak reached across the table and took her hand.

"You look beat," she said.

"I am."

She squeezed his hand. "You'll make the case. Don't worry."

 **22** The parking lot of the Stardust Hotel and Casino was full, and Eddie Sands had to park his car under an enormous billboard which faced the street. He looked up. The marquee had a ten-foot-high color cut-out of a curly-haired young comedian.

Carrying a cheap airlines flight bag—he'd picked it up at a tourist gift store on Las Vegas Boulevard—containing the counterfeit gaming chips, Eddie Sands moved through the sea of automobiles. Inside, he wandered through the busy casino to the elevator bank. He stopped where he knew he could be seen from the bar area. A minute or so later, Vito Fanducci approached him from out of the darkness of the bar. He was wearing a black sport coat and a white linen shirt buttoned at the collar. His purple birthmark looked as if it were growing from under his shirt like a disease. "Tony says you got something," Vito said.

"That's right."

He reached for the bag. "I'll take it."

Eddie Sands shook his head. "I'll give it to Tony."

"Do you know who I am?"

"You're not Tony."

Vito Fanducci stepped close to Sands. "I'm asking you a question, Slick."

"You're Vito Fanducci. Fuck you," Sands said. "Now tell Tony I want to see him."

Vito Fanducci's face became red as he glared at Sands for a moment. Then he headed toward an elevator. Without saying a word, he led Sands to Room 1487, unlocked the door, and gestured Sands inside. A shirtless Tony Parisi sat reading the newspaper on the balcony. Sands found himself staring at the yellowish flab which hung lewdly on Parisi's bloated torso.

"The feds are all over the place. I have to change rooms every couple of days to keep them off my ass," Parisi said without looking up from the newspaper. Then he slowly folded the newspaper, set it down on the table. He made a gimme gesture. Sands handed him the bag of counterfeit gaming chips. Parisi unzipped the case, reached in. He took out a handful of chips, examined them.

"This is all he had?"

"We cleaned him out," Sands said.

"The dumb shit actually believed you were the cops. This is beautiful."

"You should be able to off the chips at face value, right?" Sands said.

"Face value?" said Parisi with a look on his face as if Sands had spoken in Farsi.

"If I were you I'd have someone in the count room turn the chips to cash...slip them into the system and let the casino take the loss, right?" Sands said.

Parisi reached to an ashtray and picked up a cigar, took a wet puff, blew out smoke. "Sounds like a good idea," he said.

"There's a couple hundred grand worth of phony chips. If you turn them for full value that means we have a big pie for us to cut up. Out of my hundred grand I'll take care of Ray Beadle."

Tony Parisi gave a wry glance to Vito Fanducci. "I'm glad you got it all figured out." Vito gave Sands a condescending grin.

Sands moved deliberately to Vito. "What are you smiling at, huh, sideshow freak? Huh, motherfucker?"

Vito's grin changed into a glare.

Sands felt the familiar sense of tingling in his fingers, the flush of awareness that precedes violence, the feeling that, as a cop working a radio car, he had had at least once a day. "I don't want any of your bun-boys around when you and I talk business," Sands said without taking his eyes off Vito Fanducci.

Parisi nodded toward Vito, who glared at Sands for a moment, then turned and ambled off the balcony into the room.

Parisi looked amused. He leaned forward, tapped his cigar into the ashtray.

"It's time you and I got something straight," Sands said.

Parisi shrugged.

"I'm no longer a cop hanging around you to make a few extra bucks."

"Don't let Vito bother you, you know?"

"I went to the joint and ate months without mentioning your name. That means I passed the big test. Now we deal direct, fifty-fifty splits. That's the way I want it."

Delicately, Parisi puffed on the cigar. "I don't own this place. The casino people don't want me here. The only way I stay in business is with muscle. And muscle costs money. Maybe you forgot that in the joint?"

"If you can't down the chips maybe I should take them to somebody else."

"Certain people have to be taken care of to get the chips laid down without complications. I spread money around so that the people in the count room are covered when the hammer drops. After all that is done real nice,

I cut you in for half of whatever's left."

"And I just take your word for that?" Sands said.

"That is unless you'd rather go down to a crap table and pass 'em yourself... or drive around town peddling them for thirty percent on the dollar to junkies and whores. You wanna do that?"

Rather than answer and lose face, Sands moved to the edge of the balcony. He stared down at the ribbon of highway that was Las Vegas Boulevard. In the parking lot of the Circus Circus Casino down the boulevard, trucks and cranes were building a temporary jumping platform which he had read was to be used by a motor-cycle daredevil.

"What happened with Bruce O'Hara?" Parisi said, changing the subject.

"I changed my mind," Sands lied. "I'm not gonna hit him a second time."

"But you have the man in the jackpot."

"A rehash is too dangerous."

There was the sound of sirens in the distance: sirens in the desert.

Parisi left his seat, moved to the rail. "There's a touch that could be worth a hundred grand, maybe more, staying right here in the hotel."

"Who are we talking about?" Sands said.

"Of course, since we're equals now, if I give you the mark and the setup, then we split the shakedown money down the middle, right?" Parisi had a big, shit-eating smile.

Sands nodded.

Parisi shuffled to the sliding glass door, shoved it closed. He picked up a *Time* magazine off a lounge chair, held it up to show the cover, a portrait of a distinguished gray-haired man.

"I read his book. That's Harry Desmond."

"None other."

"What's the twist?" Sands said.

Parisi removed the cigar from his mouth. "He's a fruit. Can you imagine that? A multimillionaire who has lunch at the White House sucking a prick?" He laughed.

"How careful is he?"

"He don't troll around meeting strangers, if that's what you mean."

"What's the bait?"

"He has a chicken who works here in the hotel. A bartender. And the bartender belongs to the union. And the union belongs to my people. Isn't it nice how things work?"

"When I was on the police department, I heard the rumors that he was queer. But I also heard that he has bodyguards."

"The bodyguards aren't with him all the time."

"How do you know that?"

"Because I'm like friends with this fruit. He always asks my advice before he buys something in town."

"Where does he have his money?"

"This is the perfect part. When he's here at the Stardust, he likes to play craps. So he always carries a hundred-grand credit line at the cage. If he takes the bait, a hundred K is waiting right downstairs in the cage."

Eddie Sands walked slowly along the edge of the terrace. He turned and shook his head. "Why are you offering this to me and not one of your people?"

"You *are* one of my people."

"You know what I mean."

"Can you see Vito showing a badge?" Parisi said. He took a big puff on the cigar. "You're the expert on this shit. This is an art."

"Are you sure Desmond has a hundred grand in the jug?"

Parisi nodded. "People have checked this for me."

Sands rubbed his chin. He stood up. "I don't think I want to do it," he said. "This guy is too high-profile."

"You're talking about a hundred thousand fucking dollars," Parisi said.

"Would you go back to the joint for a hundred big ones?"

"This guy will pay like a slot machine. He's a *fruit*. If the public finds out he sucks cock he's finished. No more lunches at the White House, no more cover of *Time* magazine."

"No thanks. Too risky."

"I want you to think about it. Just think about it for a few days before you say no. I know you could pull this off with no sweat."

"Like I said."

Parisi raised his hands. "Okay, okay, I understand. But I want you to think about it."

"Let me know when you have my money."

"Huh?"

"Let me know when the chips are downed and you have my money," Sands said.

"Sure."

"I'd like you to do this Desmond thing," Parisi added as Sands left the balcony.

Sands walked through the living room, where Vito stood at the portable bar. Vito stared at him coldly. Sands stared back for a moment, then walked out.

 **23** Novak and Haynes had been summoned to Elliot's office. They left their desks and headed down the hallway.

"I'll do the talking," Novak said. "Don't let him piss you off. It's just the way he is."

"Got a sec, fellas?" Haynes said in a credible imitation of Elliot. "I've got a couple of itty-bitty questions."

They stepped into Elliot's office. Elliot, seated behind his sterile desk, smiled, waved a hand to offer chairs. "Just a couple of itty-bitty questions," he said as the agents sat down. Haynes cringed. Elliot opened a desk drawer, took out a pad and pen. "I want to be brought up to speed on the Parisi investigation."

"The bomb that killed Bruno was a pipe bomb that's impossible to trace," Novak said.

"What about the Corcoran brothers? They're bombers who work for the mob."

"They were interviewed by the Treasury boys, the ATF. They said they were playing canasta with their wives," Novak said in a businesslike manner, as if he were giving a presentation to a stranger, rather than to someone with whom he worked on a daily basis. "The wives corroborate the alibi. And no witnesses at the coffee shop could ID their photos."

Elliot wrote on his pad, cleared his throat. "Do we have any sources into Parisi? Anyone who can help us monitor what he's up to?"

Novak shook his head. "As far as the Parisi organization, Bruno was it."

Elliot shook his head sadly. "Well, we can't just throw up our hands and give up." Having made the self-evident remark, he made a point of making eye contact with Novak, then Haynes. "What have you learned about Eddie Sands?"

"We've seen him meet with Parisi," Novak said. "He has a girlfriend named Monica Brown, a con artist who's working a gold-mine scam—a daisy chain. Red talked to one of her victims."

"And the Bruce O'Hara angle?"

"He says he has no idea why Parisi would have mentioned his name."

"I think you left one itty-bitty thing out," Elliot said. "The bug and wiretap."

"Parisi didn't make any killer statements. Nothing that we could hang him with."

"Is there some reason I wasn't notified that you intended to bug Parisi's hotel room? Like, I am the attorney-in-charge of this Strike Force."

"I just forgot," Novak said, though the real reason was that he didn't want a dunce telling him what to do.

"I forgot too," Haynes said.

"I realize that under FBI and Strike Force regulations, you're not required to notify me of every investigative tactic you choose to employ, but I'm asking you as a favor to please keep me informed. This is why the Strike Force exists—to further cooperation among federal agencies in the fight against organized crime."

Novak nodded. Haynes checked his wristwatch.

Elliot fumbled through his notes. "You've spent quite a bit of time checking up on this ex-policeman, Sands. What makes you think he can do us any good?"

"He talks to Parisi. There's not that many people Parisi meets face to face."

"So you think that you might be able to make Sands work for us?"

"We're going to try."

Elliot looked down as if to check his notes. "Is there anything you've developed *of evidentiary value* that we can use against Tony Parisi?"

"Not at this point," Novak said.

"I hope you realize this is a crisis."

"Why?"

"Unless we can solve the murder of Bruno Santoro, we can never hope to persuade another witness to point the finger at Tony Parisi."

"We're doing everything we can," Novak said.

"Don't misunderstand. As far as I'm concerned I couldn't find two better men anywhere in the country to have on this investigation. But there will come a time when we'll have to pay the piper."

Haynes fidgeted at "pay the piper."

"Are you saying you don't think we're conducting an adequate investigation?" Novak said.

"Certainly not. But what I am saying is that a quarterly inspection is coming up and they may be expecting more than what we have been able to give them. The Attorney General has taken a personal interest in solving this one. If you'll remember, at the outset I insisted that the Las Vegas police not be included in the investigation—that the Strike Force handle the matter from start to finish. I stuck my neck out, risked liaison problems with the locals, so that we could handle this one on our own."

"So we're handling it," Novak said.

"I'm not criticizing either of you in any way, shape, or

form. I'm with you *one hundred and fifty percent*. But I'm not the one who calls the final shot on this. Because of the headlines Parisi has been getting lately, it may be the Attorney General himself."

"What do you think is going to happen?" Novak said.

"Frankly, I think there is a possibility that the case may be taken away from you. Reassigned. I give you my word that I would fight this *one hundred and fifty percent*, but you should be aware that with the atmospherics in Washington as they are, this could come to pass."

After the meeting, Novak and Haynes said nothing as they moved down the hallway from Elliot's office and into the squad room. Along-for-the-Ride Tyde was at his desk reading *Playboy*.

"There's word you two might get replaced on the Bruno Santoro case," Tyde said the moment they stepped foot in the door.

"Where'd you hear that?" Haynes said.

Tyde gave a furtive glance toward the hallway, opened a desk drawer, removed a piece of paper, handed it to Novak. It was a wrinkled copy of a letter typed on Department of Justice stationery. It read as follows:

TO: OC Strike Force Chief Lionel P. Chenoweth
FROM: Special-Attorney-in-Charge Ronald P. Elliot
SUBJECT: Murder of Bruno Santoro

John Novak and Garth Haynes, the FBI special agents assigned to the investigation of the car-bombing which caused the death of confidential source Bruno Santoro, have failed to come up with anything of evidentiary value whatsoever which traces back to OC target Anthony Parisi. At this time their investigation is stalled and lacks direction.

Because I see the solving of this case as the highest priority of the Las Vegas Strike Force, I ask your concurrence in replacing Novak and

Haynes. I feel that it is in the best interest of the Strike Force to do so.

Unless you object, my plan is to replace Novak and Haynes with veteran Strike Force (U.S. Customs) Special Agent Frank Tyde, who I feel will be able to inject some new impetus to the investigation. It's been my experience that often a case can be turned around 150 percent by assigning a new investigator to the case.

Though my administrative plate is more than full, I intend to work closely with Tyde in the capacity of an investigator as well as that of a prosecutor until I am able to bring this case to a successful conclusion.

I accept full responsibility for the lack of progress that has been made on this case up to the present time. Because I feel strongly that with this case rests the reputation of the Organized Crime Strike Force in the Las Vegas District, I assure you I intend to take whatever steps are necessary to bring the killer or killers to justice.

(signed) Ronald P. Elliot,
Special-Attorney-in-Charge

"Where did this memo come from?" Novak said.

"His wastebasket. I check it every day."

"Did he ask you about taking the case?"

"Not a word. And if he does, I'll immediately go on sick leave. Why should I break my ass on a case? I already have my twenty years in."

"What else have you found in his wastebasket?" Novak said.

"Nothing much. Memos for the record which make him sound like the hardest-working prosecutor in the world. Grocery lists. Shit like that."

Haynes shook his head. "That backstabbing, two-faced prick."

Novak checked his wristwatch. It was noon—time for court to recess. He removed a few sheets of blank paper from a desk drawer, stuffed them into a manila folder to take with him, and took the elevator to the second floor. There he weaved through the surge of people exiting courtrooms into the corridor and made his way to a door at the end of the hall which had a television camera mounted above it. He pressed a buzzer, looked up to the camera. The door lock snapped. He stepped into a small carpeted reception area.

From behind a polished wooden desk a young greasy-haired male clerk wearing a sport jacket with wide lapels and shoulder pads asked if he could help him.

Novak showed his ID. "John Novak," he said. "I have an affidavit for a search warrant."

The clerk looked up at a government clock on the wall, twisted his pinky ring, daintily pressed an intercom buzzer. "FBI Agent Novak is here with a search warrant."

"Send him in," said Lorraine Traynor in a perfunctory tone.

The clerk motioned to the door. Expressionless, Novak walked across the room, opened the door, and stepped into the judge's chambers. Shelves of law books covered the walls, and there was an abundance of greenery, potted and hanging plants which he knew Lorraine Traynor insisted upon caring for herself. Novak tossed the folder he was carrying into a wastebasket.

Lorraine Traynor was sitting on the floor, cross-legged, next to a pile of law books. Her judicial robe was hanging over the high-backed leather chair behind her desk. She was wearing a yellow camisole and matching skirt. "How is the bombing case going?" she said.

"It's going," Novak said. He shrugged off his suit jacket, tossed it on a sofa. "But Elliot is trying to make points with Justice by asking that Haynes and I be replaced on the investigation."

"How do you know that?"

He sat down on the carpet next to her, leaned against the bookcase. "He wrote a memo saying he intended to take personal charge of the investigation."

"Government prosecutor vying for promotion."

"You guessed it."

"Is there any way I can help?"

"Before you were appointed, you worked in the same law firm as the Attorney General, right?"

She nodded. "You want me to get the reassignment quashed."

"I wouldn't ask you."

"But it would be okay if I volunteered for the job. Right?"

Novak nodded.

"What should I say to him?"

"Tell him Elliot is a bureaucratic climber and is using the Bruno Santoro case to show off for the department. Ask him to send word to the Strike Force that he thinks it's better for the original investigators on the case to continue on."

"I should never get involved in something like this," Lorraine Traynor said. "I guess you know that."

"That's why I would never ask you."

Novak pulled her to him, kissed her fully on the lips. He tasted lipstick. "I love you," he said.

She nuzzled his shoulder. "I love to hear you say that, John. I love you too."

"I wish you weren't a judge," he said.

"I guess it would make our relationship much simpler."

"Maybe we should stop worrying about what other people think," Novak said. He released her gently, stood up, moved to the window, stared out. She followed him. He turned to her, and for a moment they just stood there looking at each other. It was still in the room; the only sound was of the traffic outside.

"I've been single for the last twelve years," he said. "My marriage lasted less than a year. I never tried to make it work, because I was an FBI hotshot and marriage was at the bottom of my list of priorities. I've changed over the years. I'm arresting the same people over and over again...for the same crimes. I guess what I'm saying is that I'm ready to..."

She touched her hand to his lips. "I've dreamed of being with you, too."

He took her hand away. "Then what are we waiting for?" he said.

She turned away from him. "We need more time with each other before we make any decisions."

"It's not that."

"I don't want us to end up hurting each other," she said.

"It's not that either," he said. "You're caught up in what other people think. You're worried that if we were married you'd have to drag a low-ranking FBI drone with you to dinner parties. 'And our guests tonight are her honor Judge Lorraine Traynor and her GS-13 husband, who is neither a legal eagle, nor a casino executive, nor some asshole who happened to be born rich.'"

"I'm sorry to hear that's what you think of our relationship," Lorraine Traynor said. She turned to face him. Their eyes met.

She had looked at him like that the first day he had testified in her court, and the time he had seen her sitting alone in a restaurant near the courthouse a few weeks later and asked if he could join her. He found himself breaking into a wry grin. She smiled.

Novak took a few steps to the door.

"Are you going?"

With his eyes on hers, he turned the latch, locked the door.

Lorraine Traynor removed her thick eyeglasses. "You're crazy," she said in a conspiratorial tone.

Novak removed his gun and handcuffs, set them on the sofa, moved across the room to her, took her in his arms. As his lips sought hers, he reached under her skirt and maneuvered his hand under her panties. Gently he massaged her. She moaned softly and spread her legs a little. As she began to clutch him tightly, he felt wetness, readiness between her legs.

"No," she whispered.

"Yes."

"I'm not going to do it here," she said.

As she tried to push him away, he dropped with her to the plush carpet. His tongue found her neck.

"You're such a pervert," she said breathlessly.

Soon, Lorraine Traynor tugged on his belt, pulled down his trousers, freed him. He rolled onto his back, lifted her violently onto him. She caught her breath and closed her eyes. She dug her nails into his forearms as he plunged into her with measured strokes, the way he knew she liked it.

She began to breathe faster.

To keep the reception clerk outside the door from wondering what was going on, they covered each other's mouth as they experienced simultaneous orgasm. Then she leaned down, rested her head on his chest, hugged him tightly.

"Don't ever do this again. I mean it," she said.

"Sorry."

She hugged him tighter.

**24** After a few minutes, they got up from the carpet and cleaned up in the bathroom which adjoined the chambers.

Novak put his gun and holster back on as Lorraine Traynor combed her hair at the mirror.

"Are you coming over Sunday?" she said. "I thought we could barbecue."

"Wouldn't miss it."

"Bring steaks."

"Yes, your honor," he said on his way out the door.

On Sunday morning, Novak rose early. He drove to the Strike Force office and let himself in. He strolled through the office to make sure no one was there. At a wall of filing cabinets, he unlocked a file drawer labeled "Parisi Organization—Closed Cases." He pulled out every file in the drawer and stacked them on his desk. He sat down, picked up one of the files, thumbed pages. Having reviewed it thoroughly, he set it aside. From the top desk drawer he took out a tablet and made brief notes.

During the next several hours, he did the same with every file he had removed from the drawer. By three o'clock he had completed his notes:

CASE TYPE	SUSPECT	DISPO
1. Extort casino mgr.	Parisi assoc.	Case dismissed
2. Beating/Taxi Union officer	Parisi assoc.	Case lost on appeal
3. Tampering/fed. witness	Parisi	Grand jury—no bill
4. Bribe police officer	Parisi assoc.	Case dismissed
5. Tax evasion	Parisi assoc.	(Nolle pros)
6. Transport stolen securities	Parisi assoc.	Susp. now fugitive
7. Interstate Trans. Aid Racketeering	Parisi	Case lost on appeal

He tore the sheet from the yellow pad, shoved it into his pocket. Novak returned the files to the filing cabinet. He checked his wristwatch. He was almost late to meet Lorraine.

On the patio of Lorraine Traynor's home, Novak dropped thick steaks on the barbecue grill. They sizzled. He picked up his third beer, took a sip.

Lorraine, who was wearing a pair of tight jeans and a halter top, sat at a redwood picnic table reading the notes he'd made at the office. Finally she handed them back to him.

"Okay. Now I know that every case against Parisi and his organization has resulted in a zero. Not one of his people has gone to jail."

"What do you make of it?" he said.

"Organized-crime cases are difficult to prosecute," she said. "Parisi has himself insulated so that no one can give direct testimony against him."

"I read every file," Novak said. "Parisi lucked out in every investigation. Either a witness backed out of testifying, or the evidence was tainted. Technicalities."

"Prosecutors make mistakes. Investigators make mistakes. People are incompetent. Incompetency is the motto of the federal government," she said.

She stood up, moved close to him, took the beer from his hand, sipped. "I thought you weren't going to take all of this so seriously anymore."

"I persuaded Bruno Santoro to talk," Novak said. "I gave him my word of honor that he would be protected. That's probably what he was thinking the moment his car blew up and he became human pizza. My promise. That makes it personal."

Novak took the meat off the grill and put it on the picnic table, which Lorraine had set with a white tablecloth and napkins. They gorged on steak, baked potatoes and salad.

"I talked to the Attorney General," Lorraine said. "I made up a reason to call, then got around to the Santoro bombing. I think he sensed I had an ulterior motive for calling, so I just came out with it. I told him that the investigators on the case should be allowed to continue."

"How did he respond?"

"He told me he knows that Elliot is a bureacratic climber and is trying to show off by offering to take over the case. And he's going to leave you and Haynes on it."

"Thanks, Lorraine. I really appreciate—"

"Eat your steak and shut up."

After dinner he helped her carry the dishes into the kitchen and put things away. "You've been preoccupied all evening, Agent Novak," Lorraine said as she closed the door to the dishwasher and turned it on.

164

"Sorry. I guess I haven't been very good company."

"I didn't mean that."

"I want to solve this case more than I've ever wanted anything else."

"Men are never satisfied. They always want to solve one more case, make one more big deal, build one more bridge."

"This isn't like pinching one more car thief."

"If Parisi disappeared tomorrow, someone else just like him would take his place."

"Maybe," Novak said. "But nevertheless this one is between him and me."

She took him by the hand. "You'll make the case," she said. They kissed passionately. He picked her up, carried her to the living-room sofa. There in the semidarkness, they undressed each other. Then they made love for a long time. Afterward, they lay in each other's arms, breathing heavily. Novak was exhausted.

Lorraine rolled over onto her back. In the dim light she looked mysterious. Dark eyes, lips, nipples.

He kissed her again.

"Please be careful," she whispered.

"I will. It would help if you could set a high bail on Monica Brown."

"Since I was a youngster my goal in life was to become a federal judge—a fair and honest judge like my father was. I scraped and scratched to make it. Now, for me to be anything other than fair and impartial in any case would be something I couldn't live with, no matter what the personal consequences."

"I'm not asking you to break any rules. The bail can be legally justified. Trust me."

She nuzzled his neck. "I'll see what I can do," she said sleepily. "I want you to stay the night. I want to be with you."

"Okay." He put his arms around her.

They woke up the next morning on the living-room floor.

• • •

Eddie Sands and Monica sat at a table near the stage of the Tiffany Showroom, a cavernous theater restaurant in the Tropicana Hotel. On the stage, a spotlight shone on a young hatchet-faced comedian attired in Italian-cut casual clothing.

"You know how you open the refrigerator and stare in looking for something to eat? Like what could change?" he said. There were a few scattered laughs. "You know how you always get a headache after watching an aspirin commercial?" Light chuckles.

"Who said this jerk was supposed to be funny?" Sands said.

"This is yuppie humor. Everything relates to television," Monica said. She gave him a playful pinch on the cheek. "You have no imagination."

"In the joint I used to imagine jumping your thighs," he whispered.

Monica leaned close, kissed him tenderly. She returned her attention to the stage.

The comedian continued. "You know the commercial with the walking raisins?"

Sands finished a drink. "This guy had to know somebody."

"That's the way it works in this town. Juice talks."

"That's the way it works everywhere. Money. The green shit. Gold. That's power."

"Sometimes you sound so cold."

After the show Sands and Monica wandered through the busy Tropicana Casino. They stopped at a crap table and Sands rolled a few numbers.

They were slightly tipsy going home. The car radio was tuned to a Las Vegas talk show whose host was interviewing Mr. Enterprise, Harry Desmond, about his plans for purchasing the Desert Inn and building a convention center on its golf course. Desmond, who had a resonant Clark Gable voice, spoke confidently.

"My experience as a member of the Federal Reserve Board taught me that in this day and age the development of new jobs and capital is the responsibility of men like myself. One day I just realized that entrepreneurship was really where the buck stopped. Risk-taking was what started Las Vegas."

"I understand you are considering entering the entertainment field, also," the host said.

"When I complete the Las Vegas projects I intend to make an offer to purchase one of the major movie studios. I'm going to see to it that more good old-fashioned family-style entertainment gets on the air. You see, I'm a risk-taker and a family man...and damn proud of being both."

"There's some reason why Tony wants me to shake down Desmond," Sands said. "The Desmond play has been there all this time, and all of a sudden he wants to give it to *me*, knowing that I get half. Doesn't make sense."

"Maybe he looks at you as the expert at shakedowns. He wants it done right."

"That's what he said," Sands mused.

Monica touched his thigh. "I don't want you to do anything dangerous, Eddie."

"Desmond is a tempting play. I could go back to him more than once."

"Why is Tony stalling on paying you for the chips?"

"I don't like it either," Sands said. "He has the juice to dump the chips for face value anytime he wants to."

"Of course, everybody stalls when it comes to money."

Sands slowed down with the traffic. "I was a cop for a lot of years, hon. I learned that most things in life are exactly what they appear to be. That's the difference between me and the suckers that send you their money."

"You mean you see things clearer."

"I mean I know the difference between chicken salad and chicken shit."

She laughed softly. "My suckers are all so greedy. I play to the greed." She covered her mouth as she yawned and laid her head on his shoulder. There was nothing but the sound of tires on pavement. "Sometimes I get tired...tired of everything. Like maybe there's some other way."

"You've had too much wine," Sands said as he pulled up to a stoplight near the Thunderbird Casino. The casino's facade, a million-watt display in the shape of a huge silver bird, flashed intermittent daylight. The signal light changed. He drove on.

"Sometimes I think I'd like to get out of this town," she said. "We could move away."

"What would we do?"

"I could sell real estate in L.A. My clients would be Arab sheiks, rich Jews. There are million-dollar deals done every day in Malibu, Beverly Hills."

"And I could work as a security guard for three bucks an hour," he said sarcastically. "It'd be a great life."

"Leo knows I'm the one who set him up."

"Leo is a piece of shit. He's probably still in Nassau waiting for Ray and me."

"One of our deals could backfire," she said.

"Whatever happens, I'll handle it."

She turned to him. "I love you, Eddie," she said as a statement of fact.

Without slowing down, he reached out, pulled her close to him.

Back at the apartment, they held hands on the way up the stairs. Sands unlocked the door. They stepped inside into darkness. Playfully, Monica reached between his legs, pulled him close to her. Their tongues met.

John Novak, who stood near the door, touched the light switch. Sands whirled in a fighter's stance. Monica shrieked. Novak showed his badge. He kept a hand on his gun as Red Haynes shoved the door closed, frisked Sands efficiently.

"You people have a warrant to be in here?" Sands said.

Novak took his hand off his gun, reached into his suit jacket, and pulled out a legal-size document. He handed it to Sands. Sands examined the paper. He read: "Search warrant for items relating to wire and mail fraud committed by Monica Brown." Sands showed the document to Monica. Her jaw dropped.

"What does this mean?" Monica said.

"We've completed our search," Novak said as he nodded to the kitchen table. "We found the telephone and banking records we were looking for."

"What is this all about?" Monica said.

"It means we have evidence on the phone scams you've been pulling," Novak said.

"Am I under arrest?"

"Why don't we sit down?" Novak said. Sands and Monica looked at each for a moment, then quietly moved toward the table.

As Monica sat down, Novak noticed she was shaking.

They took seats at the table. Warily, Haynes leaned against the wall.

"Eddie's familiar with our operation," Novak said to Monica. "We're working a case on someone he knows."

"Just exactly what is this all about?" Monica said.

"Tony Parisi," Novak said.

"Tony Parisi?" Monica said. "I've never even *heard* of Tony Parisi. I mean, I've read about him in the newspaper, but I've never so much as—"

"Sometimes we get a little far afield in our investigations," Novak interrupted, "but some way or another things usually get back on track. Sometimes it depends on what's at stake...what's at stake for those concerned." Novak was staring directly at Sands.

Monica fidgeted, picked at her face.

"Our main job is finding people who know Parisi... potential witnesses, like Eddie here, who might be willing to testify for the government."

"Do you have an arrest warrant for Monica?" Sands said after a long silence.

"We didn't want to have an arrest warrant issued until we could talk with the two of you. But we have a solid felony case...a slam dunk."

"A case for what?"

"Fraud by wire," Novak said. "Monica scammed a nice old lady named Mabel Kincaid out of her savings. Because she used the telephone in the commission of the crime, it's a violation of federal law."

Monica fidgeted again. "So help me God I've never heard that name before in my life. And I swear I've never scammed anybody out of anything. I don't know what the hell you're talking about. Eddie, what *is* this?"

Sands maintained eye contact with Novak. "When I was a cop, sometimes I used to bullshit people into giving me information. I would tell them I had a case on someone when actually I didn't have shit."

Novak nodded at Red Haynes. Haynes, wearing a Cheshire-cat smile, reached into his coat pocket, pulled out a small tape player, set it upright on the table between the two men. He pressed the play button. There was static, then the sound of a phone ringing, the click of a receiver.

"Nevada Gold Mining Trust. Monica Butler speaking."

"This is Mabel Kincaid."

Monica folded her hands. "That was a perfectly legitimate investment opportunity," she said. "I can explain."

"Okay, you have a case," Sands cut in.

Haynes pressed the off button on the tape player. Monica bit her lip, turned to stare at the wall.

"They don't really care about you," Sands said without taking his eyes off Novak. "They're here to hammer me."

Neither Novak nor Haynes said anything.

Sands pushed his chair back, stood up. Haynes moved from his place by the wall as Sands paced a few feet. He stopped. "What happens now?" he said.

"We leave with the evidence . . . and unless something happens to make us change our mind, next Wednesday, when the grand jury meets, we indict Monica. Three felony counts of fraud by wire. She'll have to do some time."

"And if I agree to testify against Parisi you'll forget about the case against her?"

"We can't make any promises," Novak said.

"That would be unethical," Haynes chimed in.

Sands folded his arms across his chest. "But if I testified, her case might suddenly be dismissed, right?"

Casually, Novak straightened his necktie. "That's a safe bet. A very safe bet."

Sands stared at Monica for a moment. He turned to Novak. "I need a few days to think about it."

Novak stood up. He nodded at Red Haynes. Haynes reached into his back pocket, pulled out handcuffs. He motioned for Monica to stand up.

"You're going to book her?" Sands said.

"That's right. You can let me know if you change your mind," Novak said. Haynes snapped handcuffs onto Monica's wrists, led her to the door. Novak picked up the evidence on the table.

"What's the bail?" Sands said.

Novak moved to the door. He stopped. "The bail hasn't been set," he said.

"I'll have you out as soon as the bail is set, hon," Sands said as Haynes led the frightened Monica past him and out the door.

"I know what you're doing," Sands said.

"You can ask around about me," Novak said. "I'm known as a man of my word. If you testify truthfully in front of a grand jury, Monica walks. That promise won't be written down in any report, nor will I ever admit to having made it. But it's exactly what will happen."

"I don't know much about Parisi anyway."

"Then why not take the stand and say just that?"

"Because once I begin to testify you can get me for perjury. I know that game," Sands said.

"Not if you're telling the truth."

"The cemetery is full of federal snitches," Sands said.

Novak shrugged. "And the penitentiary is full of prisoners," he said. Then he left.

．　．　．

Eddie Sands, feeling clammy and slightly nauseated, watched through the window as the agents led Monica past a streetlight to a sedan. At the sink, he turned on the faucet, filled a glass with water. He drank, set the glass down on the countertop. In his memory he felt Monica's hands wrap around him from behind.

 **25** The next morning, Sands sat in Courtroom Three at the federal courthouse. At the defense table, Monica conferred in low tones with the on-duty federal public defender, a fragile-looking young man with a wispy beard and spectacles. Elliot sat at the prosecution table.

There was the sound of a buzzer.

A husky bailiff wearing a shiny blue sport coat with a U.S. marshal's badge affixed to the breast pocket stood up. "All rise." As those in the courtroom came to their feet, the chamber door opened. The judge, a well-groomed woman whom Sands remembered as a defense attorney trying cases at the county courthouse when he was with the police department, entered the courtroom.

"This United States District Court is now in session," the bailiff said. "The Honorable Lorraine C. Traynor presiding. Please be seated."

The judge took the bench. Sands sat down.

Judge Traynor referred to some papers in front of her. "Case Number 95756, Monica Brown, for the setting of bail," Traynor said.

The public defender stood up. "Lyman B. Kabekoff for the office of the public defender present as counsel for the defendant Brown, your honor."

"Good morning," Traynor said.

The prosecutor stood up. "Ronald Elliot for the government, your honor."

"Very well," she said without looking up from the papers in front of her. "The court has reviewed the financial statement prepared by the defendant, her arrest record, and an affidavit signed by FBI Agent..." She referred to the affidavit in front of her. "Uh... Agent Novak," she said, "which reflects the probable cause for the arrest. Mr. Kabekoff, would you like to be heard?"

Kabekoff rose. "Your honor, the recommendation of no bail in this case is not based on any facts which tend to show that this defendant will not make all of her required court appearances. I submit that the defendant is a longtime resident of this community and has never been convicted of a felony crime."

Judge Traynor turned to Elliot. "Mr. Elliot."

Elliot stood up. "Your honor, the government stands by the recommendation of no bail. This defendant is involved in a scheme to defraud the elderly and others of their life savings. She was the subject of an investigation concerning a similar crime six years ago and apparently has not changed her ways. The government considers her a danger to the community, and because of her obvious access to false identification, which she uses to perpetrate her schemes, she is a definite flight risk."

Kabekoff asked to be heard again. Judge Traynor nodded.

"Your honor, this is the same litany we always hear when the Organized Crime Strike Force appears at a

174

bail hearing. This defendant is not a danger to anyone, and, in fact, has a history of making all her court appearances."

Judge Traynor removed her eyeglasses. "Does the government have anything to add?"

Elliot stood up. "This defendant uses various false identities, your honor...business fronts, mail drops," he said.

"Thank you, Mr. Elliot," she said. Elliot sat down, folded his hands.

"Very well," she said. "The court finds that the government has not made a sufficient showing to prove this defendant a danger to the community. Thus, the government's recommendation of no bail is denied....But it also finds that the defendant has access to false identification, is not regularly employed, and has an arrest record which reflects sophisticated fraud activity involving the use of counterfeit documents and business fronts. These factors lead the court to deem the defendant a potential flight risk. Therefore, a corporate surety bond is considered appropriate."

Taken aback, Kabekoff rose slowly from his chair.

"Bail is set in the amount of five hundred thousand dollars' corporate surety," she said. "The clerk will call the next case."

"Thank you, your honor," Elliot said. The bailiff moved toward Monica.

Kabekoff sprang to attention. "Your honor. May I be heard, your honor?"

"Do you have something *new* to add to the case at hand, Mr. Kabekoff?"

"Your honor. Five hundred thousand dollars?"

"Do you have anything new to add to this matter, Mr. Kabekoff?"

"No. No, your honor."

"Then this matter is concluded. The clerk will call the next case."

As she was led toward the door to the holding area, Monica's eyes were on Sands. Sands moved toward the

175

rail. The bailiff opened the door to the holding area, ushered her inside.

Sands hurried to the courtroom door, caught up with Kabekoff. "I want you to appeal that bail," Sands said.

"I knew there was something fishy as soon as I saw a Strike Force attorney standing there for a routine bail setting," Kabekoff said. "But five hundred thousand dollars? Outrageous! They're trying to squeeze her for information."

"I want you to appeal," Sands said.

"I will. But I have five other cases to handle today before I get around to the paperwork. And I must tell you, this judge said the right things to make the bail stick."

"Shit," Sands said.

"Didn't you use to be on the police department?" Kabekoff said as Eddie Sands left the courtroom.

The street was one Eddie Sands was familiar with.

He climbed out of his car and moved briskly down the sidewalk, past dingy storefronts—an office of a lawyer who, Sands knew, dealt a little cocaine to supplement his income, a professional debt-collection agency whose employees used phony names when dealing with the public, a twenty-four-hour-a-day marriage chapel whose fly-specked bay window displayed a soiled, heart-shaped satin pillow resting on a stand, a Western Union office that reportedly did the largest money-order business of any in the world.

The office next door to the marriage chapel had burglar-alarm tape around the perimeter of its bay window and flaking gold letters which read "Joey Giambra—Bail Bonds." Sands opened the door, entered. The tiny office, which had nothing in it except a desk, a gray metal filing cabinet, a couple of chairs, and an oversized racehorse calendar on the wall, smelled of stale cigar smoke. The place was the way Sands remembered it. Joey Giambra, a diminutive middle-aged man with a waxy stayed-up-all-night complexion, was sitting at the desk.

176

"Eddie Sands. I used to be with the department."

Without standing up, the expressionless Giambra gave Sands a weak handshake. "I remember you," he said. "Intelligence. Your partner was Ray Beadle." He nodded to a chair. Sands sat down.

"I've got a problem," Sands said.

"Most people do who come here."

"The FBI arrested my wife on a humbug... something about a fraud. It's a nothing deal. But they set a high bond on her because they're trying to squeeze me."

"How much are we talking about?"

"Five hundred thou."

"Five hundred? Which judge set it?" he asked, his loose false teeth making a clacking sound.

"Judge Traynor."

"She doesn't set 'em like that very often." Giambra's lack of expression changed into a sardonic smile. Using his thumbs, he pushed his upper dental plate back into position.

"I'm told you're the only bondsman in town who can handle a bond that big."

Giambra picked up a pen and a pad of paper. "How much cash you got?"

"Thirty-five grand."

Giambra noted the amount on the pad. "How much property?"

"No property."

"No property? Cars?"

"No cars."

"Jewelry?"

Sands shook his head.

Giambra set the pen down. "Looks like we're about four hundred and sixty-five thousand dollars short of collateral."

"I didn't come here to talk about any fucking collateral. My wife is in jail and I want her out."

Giambra tore off the sheet of paper, crumpled it, then threw it into a wastebasket. "Can't risk it," he clacked.

"I was a cop in this town. You've seen me around for years."

"If I post a yard and your old lady decides not to show up for trial I'm outta business."

"You have my word she'll show up. You can ask about me. The people know me."

Giambra stood up, adjusted his crotch. "If Eddie Sands is solid with the people, then he should have no problem getting a cosigner for the bond. Or you can wait for an appeal. Bonds get lowered eventually."

"I want her out. I want her out right now."

Giambra's wax mask made an expression that meant he had heard it all before, a thousand times. "I bet it's strange for you to be on the other side like this. I mean, after all the people you arrested."

Sands stood up as his anger welled. Joey Giambra stopped smiling as Sands moved closer to him. "Nothing personal," Giambra said. "You know how it is in this town. One day a guy's a headliner, the next day he's a friggin' lounge show. Nothing personal."

Without saying anything, Eddie Sands turned away.

"If you get something together, come back and see me," Giambra said.

Down the street at the modern twelve-story building that was the Las Vegas City Jail, Sands showed his driver's license to a deputy sheriff, filled in a visitors form. The deputy pointed down a hallway to a door marked "Visitors." He made his way into the room. There were nine fixed metal stools facing a bulletproof glass partition. Only one was not occupied. He sat down and waited.

About fifteen minutes later Monica came to the window. She sat down across from him. Her hair was matted and she wore no makeup. As they picked up telephones, he noticed that the green prison gown she was wearing was fully two sizes too large for her.

"Are you okay?" he said and immediately realized that the question sounded stupid.

Rather than answering his question, she just stared blankly at him. Her chin quivered. She ran a hand through her hair, took a deep breath in order to compose herself. "Can you get the bail lowered?"

"It'll take some time," he said.

Monica covered her eyes for a moment. She wiped tears.

"*Murderers* don't get bonds that high."

"The feds are doing this to make me talk," Sands said.

Monica Brown took a Kleenex from the pocket of her smock. She wiped her nose. "I know this sounds crazy, but I want to ask you a question."

"Go, hon."

"Is there anything you can give them?" she said. "I know you could never be a snitch or anything like that, but isn't there some information you could give them about Parisi that could have come from somewhere else?"

"Answering one question leads to answering another. It would never work."

"I can't sleep or eat in here. This place is full of dykes."

"I'm gonna get you out," he said.

"Please don't do anything crazy to get me out of here."

"I want you to relax, hon. I'll have you out of here in a day or two."

"I love you, Eddie."

"I love you too," Eddie Sands said. He felt like breaking through the glass with his hands and pulling her to him.

Sands moved along the sidewalk to his car. He stopped, looked back at the jail. He ran his hands through his hair a couple of times, then wandered across the street and into a bar. There were no customers in the place. A gray-haired bartender approached. Sands ordered a double shot of whiskey. The bartender poured the drink, set it on a cocktail napkin. Sands downed it.

The whiskey burned his tongue and the back of his throat. His eyes watered.

"You okay, buddy?" the bartender said.

Sands didn't answer. After a while, he set money on the bar to pay for the drink. From a pay phone just inside the door, he dialed the number of the Stardust Hotel. When the operator came on the line he asked for Tony Parisi.

 **26** It was midday.

Eddie Sands, with the air conditioner in the car on high, waited in the parking lot of the Desert Inn golf course. He had parked in a space next to a tall wire-mesh fence which paralleled the course, giving him a view of both the entrance to the parking lot and the palm-lined course itself. He checked his wristwatch again, watched a golf cart full of garishly dressed golfers cruise past a sand trap.

Parisi was late.

After a while, a Cadillac pulled into the parking lot. As it cruised toward him he recognized Parisi in the driver's seat. The Cadillac pulled into the space next to him.

Tony Parisi climbed out. He looked around cautiously, flicked ashes from his cigar, then motioned to Sands.

Sands got out and joined him. Together, they began walking along the fence.

"What's the big emergency?" Parisi said.

"The feds arrested Monica on wire fraud."

"What's the bail?"

"Five hundred grand."

"You should be able to get it lowered."

"I tried, but the judge, some woman named Traynor, won't go for it," Sands said.

"What are you gonna do?"

Sands stopped walking. Parisi turned to face him.

"I . . . uh . . . I want you to go the bail for her."

"Five hundred large? Get serious."

"One phone call and a bondsman would do it for you. You have the juice to get her out."

Tony Parisi looked at his cigar, then at the golf course. "Like the wise man said, what the fuck is in it for me?"

"I'll shake down Harry Desmond for you. You said he's good for a hundred thousand. It'll be all yours."

"If Monica doesn't show for court, then I owe the bondsman five hundred."

"You have my word she'll show up for court. You'll make a hundred grand on the deal."

Tony Parisi gave him a condescending smile. "This broad means a lot to you, doesn't she?"

"You stand to make a hundred grand," Sands said, ignoring the comment.

Parisi bared his teeth as he puffed his cigar, emitted smoke slowly for a moment, then blew it all out. "When will you be ready to shake Desmond?"

"I'm ready right now."

"I'll arrange that Desmond's bodyguard won't be with him tomorrow night," Parisi said. "And I'll see to it that the people in the cashier's cage at the Stardust don't ask a lot of questions if Desmond makes any special requests." Parisi stared at the golf course. He puffed on his cigar.

"I need to meet the decoy," Sands said.

"His name is Skippy. He works station three at the

casino bar. I'll prime him to expect a visit from you."

Nothing else was said as they walked back toward the cars. Parisi reached into his right trouser pocket. He pulled out a master key for the Stardust Hotel, handed it to Eddie Sands. "Bring this and the hundred grand back to me and I'll have Monica bailed out in an hour," Parisi said. He opened the door of the Cadillac, climbed in, lowered the window, stuck out his hand. "Good luck, kid," he said. They shook hands.

Sands was surprised that even on such a hot day Parisi's hand was completely dry and cool.

After the meeting with Sands, Tony Parisi drove down the Strip a few blocks. He turned right and, a block or so down the road, pulled into a supermarket parking lot, parked, turned off the engine. He sat for a moment keeping his eye on the driveway entrance to the parking lot until he was satisfied that no one had followed him.

He climbed out of the Cadillac, made his way across the parking lot to a bank of pay phones near the entrance. He pulled a slip of paper from his wallet. It had Mickey Greene's phone number on it. He dropped change and dialed. Greene's secretary came on the line. He gave his name. The line clicked.

"Hello, my friend," Mickey Greene said.

"I've found that boat you were looking for," Parisi said. "The owner is in town. But I don't know for how long. Are you still interested in buying?"

Nothing was said for a moment. Finally, Mickey Greene cleared his throat. "Absolutely. We're talking about the same price?"

"If you want the boat the price is doubled. You want to discuss it with your people and call me back?"

"We'll pay the price."

"Then you're telling me to go ahead with the deal?"

"Go ahead. It's a definite go."

"He expects a down payment soon," Parisi said.

"I'm coming over for the weekend."

"That should work out fine."

Then, without saying anything further, Tony Parisi set the phone back on the hook. He relit his cigar and stood there for a moment wondering what he would eat for lunch. Having decided on steak, he blew a little smoke and headed back to his car.

That night, in the Stardust Casino, Eddie Sands sidled up to the bar. The bartender approached. Sands noticed that his face was lightly sprayed with pockmarks, a feature he hadn't noticed before, probably because of the lack of light in the bar. "Are you Skippy?" he asked.

"I thought you might be the one Tony told me about," Skippy said. "I've seen you before." Eddie Sands didn't offer his hand. Nervously, Skippy folded his arms across his chest.

"When's the last time you were with Harry Desmond?"

"I'm nervous about this whole thing, man."

"Didn't Tony tell you to trust me?'"

"He said that you would handle everything. But I can't help being jumpy."

"Relax, Skippy. I just have a couple of questions."

"You're just like a cop. I mean like really."

"How about a little scotch?" Sands said. Skippy picked up a glass and a metal scoop. Expertly, he loaded the scoop with ice, dropped it into a glass. He poured a drink, set it in front of Sands. Sands took a little sip. "When did you first meet Desmond?"

"I worked some private cocktail parties he had in one of the suites. Afterward, when everyone else was gone, we just talked. He said he had trouble sleeping. I could tell he wanted to . . ."

"So now you're close," Sands said. "How does he let you know when he wants to get together?"

"He calls me at the bar. Or sometimes he comes down. He wears dark glasses around the hotel because people recognize him. He gets interviewed on a lot of TV shows."

"When you and he get together," Sands said, "does he have you come to his room?"

Skippy pursed his lips and shook his head. "Never," he said. "He's very discreet. He doesn't want to be seen with a . . . gay. He rents a room for us on another floor."

"Exactly what is the procedure?" Sands said in an impatient tone.

"He'll call me at the bar and ask if I can get away for an hour. I say yes. He comes down to the bar and stands at the elevators over there. I leave the bar and we both get on the same elevator. I get off at the floor he does and follow him to a room. Sometimes he won't even go into the room if there's other people in the hall. Like I say, he's ultra-discreet. Ultra-closet."

"How does he pay you?"

"Cash."

"The cash . . . does he take it out of a wallet?"

"Yes."

"What kind of a wallet is it?"

Skippy picked up a bottle, poured himself a drink. "It's a long one. Like a checkbook wallet."

"Is there a checkbook in the wallet?"

"I think so. Yeah, I'm pretty sure."

"How often does he usually want to see you when he stays here?" Sands said.

"Once a day. Usually in the middle of the evening," Skippy said with a wry smile. "He finds me irresistible. See, I'm Portuguese. And he told me he loves Portuguese men."

Eddie Sands sipped scotch. "Is there any way you could take a look at his checkbook without him knowing it?"

"He always showers after. He's a cleanliness nut."

"Tonight, if you can do it without any problem, I want you to get me one of his checks. Just one. Take it out of the back of the checkbook, not the front."

"No problem. Then what?"

"We'll talk again tomorrow morning."

 **27** The next morning, Sands had breakfast at the Desert Inn. Though it was an all-you-can-eat buffet, he only picked at his food. He had slept fitfully most of the night, and he had a headache.

Skippy the bartender, wearing white trousers and a windbreaker, entered from the casino, spotted Sands, and headed for the table. He sat down. Sands thought he looked rested.

"How did everything go?" Sands said.

Skippy looked around, reached into his windbreaker, took out a racing form. He handed it to Sands. Discreetly, Sands looked at the opened form. Inside was a personal check which was imprinted:

HARRY DESMOND
MR. ENTERPRISE INC.
Personal Account

"You did good, Skippy," Sands said.

Skippy smiled. "That's what Harry said, too." He let out a high-pitched laugh.

Sands removed a ballpoint pen from his shirt pocket, handed it and the racing form containing the check back to Skippy. "I want you to make out the check to...uh... the Desert Inn for six thousand dollars. Sign Desmond's name."

"Can I get in trouble for doing this?"

"This is something Tony Parisi wants you to do, Skippy. Would you like him to tell you in person?"

Skippy complied, then handed the pen and the racing form containing the check back to Sands. Sands shoved the items into his inside coat pocket.

"Can you tell me exactly what is going to happen?" Skippy said.

"You just do your thing again tonight. Make sure he stops by the bar to pick you up. In the room it's better if both you and he have no clothes on."

"That's no problem. He makes me strip the moment we walk in the door. He can't wait to get *down*."

"I want you to relax and just react the way you would if something like this were to really happen."

"The whole thing isn't going to work, you know," Skippy said.

"What makes you say that?"

"When we leave the bar you won't know what room we're going to."

"That's where the toothpicks come in."

"Toothpicks?"

That night, Sands and Beadle, dressed in business suits, stood near a bank of slot machines watching the bar and the nearby bank of elevators. Because a dinner show had just gotten out, the casino was crowded. Beadle reached into his coat, took out a clear plastic envelope which was marked with a stick-on evidence tag, handed it to Sands. Sands took Desmond's check from his shirt pocket, slipped it into the evidence envelope, sealed the flap. He slid the envelope into his jacket pocket.

"My sorry ass is nervous as hell," Beadle said.

"That's part of it," Sands said without taking his eyes off the elevators.

"Very funny."

The elevator doors opened. A gray-haired man wearing dark glasses stepped off, moved toward the bar. It was Harry Desmond.

At the bottom of the carpeted steps leading to the bar area, Desmond stopped, shuffled about for a moment until Skippy noticed him. Their eyes met immediately. Desmond moved back to the elevator bank. Skippy said something to the other bartender, ducked under the bar. He hurried to the hall, where a small group had gathered to wait for an elevator. Neither man spoke. When an elevator arrived, Desmond and Skippy got on along with the others.

Sands and Beadle hurried to the elevator bank. They watched the light above the elevator door as it moved horizontally from number to number. The elevator was stopping at almost every floor. Another elevator arrived. The doors opened. They stepped in. Sands pushed the button for the second floor. The elevator ascended. He and Beadle stepped off, inspected the carpet outside the elevator. Nothing. They stepped back in the elevator and proceeded to the next floor. There they checked again.

They repeated this procedure nine times.

On the eleventh floor, Sands spotted a few toothpicks lying on the carpet outside the elevator. He motioned to Beadle. They separated, moved different ways along the hallway, checking near each door. As Sands reached the center of the hallway, Beadle made a *pssst* sound. Sands headed back in his direction. Beadle, looking pale and nervous, pointed to the threshold of Room 1198. There were four or five toothpicks on the carpet in front of the door.

Having glanced both ways to see that no one else was

in the hallway, Sands placed his ear to the door. There were muffled sounds he couldn't make out. He pulled the master key from his pocket. Making as little noise as possible, he eased the key in, turned. The lock clicked. He shoved the door violently.

Sands and Beadle ran into the room. A nude Skippy was perched on the end of the bed. Harry Desmond, also naked, was kneeling at his feet, blowing him.

"Police officers!" Sands said.

Harry Desmond made an animal yelp as Skippy pulled away.

Beadle grabbed Skippy by the arm, flashed a badge. "You're under arrest for forgery, clown. Get some clothes on."

Harry Desmond, in the manner of an embarrassed child, turned toward the wall, covered himself.

"There must be some mistake, officer," Skippy said, probably because he'd heard someone say it in a movie.

Beadle shoved him backward onto a pile of clothes on the bed. "I said get dressed, asshole."

"Okay, okay," Skippy said. He picked up a pair of trousers and began to dress.

"Let's see some ID," Sands said to Harry Desmond, who was still facing the wall. He was shaking.

"I'm ... Harry Desmond. May I get dressed?"

"Oh. Mr. Desmond. Sure," Sands said.

Avoiding eye contact with Sands, Harry Desmond stepped to the dresser. He kept his head down as he quickly slid his skinny legs into his trousers, shrugged on his shirt. "I think we'd better talk in private, Mr. Desmond," Sands said.

Desmond stared at Sands for a moment; he looked as if he was going to faint. Sands nodded toward the bathroom. As Desmond reluctantly followed him in, Ray Beadle snapped handcuffs on Skippy.

Sands closed the door. The bathroom walls were mirrors. "We had no idea you would be here, Mr. Desmond. I'm ... uh ... sorry."

"What is happening?" Harry Desmond said. Carefully, he lowered himself onto the edge of the bathtub.

Sands reached inside his suit jacket, pulled out the clear plastic envelope containing the check Skippy the bartender had given him, and showed it to Desmond. Desmond reached out to take it. Sands pulled it back. "Sorry, sir. It's evidence."

"Where did you get that check?"

"Skippy has been forging your checks all over Las Vegas. The total is up to nineteen thousand dollars."

"I didn't even know I had checks missing."

"The bank caught it. The signatures were dissimilar. We traced him back here, followed him to this room."

"What's going to happen now?"

"We book Skippy for forgery and write a report," Sands said. "As the victim, I'm afraid you'll have to come down to the office with us."

"I don't want this to go any further. They're my checks. I choose not to file a complaint."

"It's not that easy, Mr. Desmond," Sands said. "The bank has been in touch with your business manager in Beverly Hills. He said he wanted the forger arrested. A complaint was signed on your behalf."

Desmond turned to Sands. "Uh...this is all a misunderstanding. I want to end this right here," he pleaded.

"We've just made a legal arrest and placed a man in handcuffs," Sands said. "We can't just take the cuffs off, walk away, and forget it. I have to write a report and—"

"Officer, if we go down to your office this whole matter will make the newspapers. I insist that you release the man in the other room and drop the charges. *Do you understand that?*"

"Sir, a felony crime has been committed," Sands said. "There are certain things I'm required to do."

Desmond, gathering his executive composure, stood up, took a deep breath. "Officer, I am a personal friend of the governor of this state. I know every politician in this city by his first name. I think it would be best for you to just let this matter drop."

"I understand your...uh...sense of embarrassment, Mr. Desmond, but this isn't just some minor business deal you can turn your back on," Sands said. "This is a matter of law. As a law-enforcement officer I have certain responsibilities. If I don't carry them out and the police department finds out, then *I* get embarrassed. Or maybe fired."

Harry Desmond shook his head. "I'm not going to leave this room. I've committed no crime."

"Mr. Desmond, I'm trying to be reasonable with you. But don't push it too far."

Desmond used the back of his hand to wipe a fine line of perspiration from his upper lip. "I hope you realize who you are dealing with."

"To me, you're nothing but a run-of-the-mill queer."

"If I refuse to make a complaint you have no right to arrest anyone," Desmond said, ignoring the remark. "I'm not going anywhere with you."

Sands closed the cover on the toilet. He sat down, faced Harry Desmond. Because of the mirrors in the room, there were reflections of both of them from all angles. He glared at Desmond. "You'll come with me. One way or the other."

Desmond made a funny sound as he tried, but failed, to clear his throat. "I apologize if I sounded hostile, officer," he said. "But can't you just walk out of here and leave me alone?"

"Yes, I can. I also can throw handcuffs on you and book you into the queen tank at the county jail. The bottom line is, what's in it for me and my partner?"

Harry Desmond swallowed, cleared his throat. "This whole thing is a setup. You waited until you knew he was coming to be with me."

"Even if we did, it doesn't change your predicament, does it?" Sands said.

"I'd like to discuss alternatives."

"There are only three alternatives. One, we book jocko in there for hanging paper and you for sodomy.

Two, we just book jocko and write a report which lists you as the victim. Three, in order to avoid publicity, my partner and I stick our necks out and try to sweep this whole incident under the table."

"I would appreciate any consideration you could offer."

"The price is a hundred grand," Sands said. "That's fifty for my partner and fifty for me. Any less and it's not worth the risk."

"Now I get it," Desmond said with a tinge of weakness in his voice. The perspiration had reappeared around his mouth. "This is nothing more than a shakedown. Blackmail."

"You're a big businessman. I'll bet you've squeezed a few sacks yourself on the way up."

Harry Desmond stared at his reflection in the facing mirror for a while. "Blackmail goes against everything I stand for," he said.

Sands stood up, yanked handcuffs off his belt. "In that case, let's go to jail, fucker."

Desmond stared at the handcuffs. "I'll pay each of you ten thousand dollars."

"This is Las Vegas," Sands said. "The big town. People playing keno win more than that every hour downstairs in the casino."

"I want to make a phone call."

Sands laughed. "To who? To your wife and kids so you can tell them you're gay? Or maybe to your board of directors?"

"I ask this as a favor."

"Fuck your favor. You have one minute to make up your mind, then it's time to get booked for oral cop."

"What about the people at the bank?" Desmond said.

"Sir?"

"You said you talked about the stolen checks to the people at the bank."

"I'll talk to 'em again. This time I tell 'em the investigation showed your checks were from an old checkbook you'd thrown away. A Mexican guy found the checks in a trash can, forged a few of them, then returned to Mexico. Since there's no extradition treaty with Mexico for the crime of forgery, the case is closed."

Desmond stared at himself in the mirror. Tears welled in his eyes. Eddie Sands stifled the urge to cheer. He lit a cigarette, tossed the match in the bathtub.

Mr. Enterprise's chin quivered for a moment. "If I pay a hundred thousand, how will I be guaranteed this... uh...incident will never come to light?"

"Because I don't want to go to jail for soliciting a bribe any more than you want your biography to be titled *Call Me Jocko*."

Harry Desmond looked at himself in the mirror for a moment. "No."

"No what, Mr. Desmond?"

"I'm not going to pay," he said, watching Sands carefully.

Without hesitation, Sands pulled his gun. "Then you're under arrest. Put your hands on top of your head."

Desmond's complexion turned pale. His chin quivered mightily. Finally he broke into uncontrollable sobs. His hands covered his face and he dropped to his knees on the bathroom floor. "Okay, I'll *pay*."

Eddie Sands smiled. "Where is your money?" he said.

Harry Desmond slowed his sobbing, looked up, wiped his eyes and nose with his right hand.

"The Chase Manhattan Bank—"

"This isn't some blue-chip stock trade," Sands said impatiently. "I mean money we can put our hands on right this minute."

"I have credit here at the casino."

Sands led Desmond into the other room. Ray Beadle was standing in the middle of the room with the handcuffed Skippy. He feigned writing in a small notebook. "Take him to the car," Sands said. Beadle put the notebook away, led Skippy toward the door.

As they went out, Sands picked up the phone receiver. "You were in a poker game with some pals," he said. "You need a hundred grand to cover your losses and you'll pick it up at the casino cage." He handed the receiver to Desmond and dialed the number of the casino count room.

28 The elevator doors opened onto the casino. Harry Desmond, wearing his dark glasses, stepped off, Eddie Sands behind him.

In the casino, Sands watched from behind a row of slot machines as Desmond approached the cashier's cage. A bushy-haired man with thick glasses came to the counter. After a brief discussion, the man left. He returned shortly from the count room with a package wrapped in brown paper. Harry Desmond signed a form. The man handed Desmond the package. Awkwardly, Desmond looked about, then headed straight past the gaming tables and out the side door of the casino.

Sands followed.

Outside in the parking lot, which was full because of a convention being held at the hotel, Sands continued behind Desmond at a discreet distance until he was sure no one had followed them from the casino. Then he picked up his pace, caught up with Desmond, and took the package out of his hands. "Go back inside," Sands said.

"What about Skippy?"

"He'll be released," Sands said. "There will be no police report. You're free to go."

"Thank you, officer."

"Sergeant."

"Thank you, sergeant."

Harry Desmond walked slowly back toward the casino.

Ray Beadle approached Sands.

"Where's Skippy?" Sands said without taking his eyes off Desmond.

"His sorry fruit ass is long gone, partner."

Harry Desmond entered the side door of the casino without looking back.

"Wait here," Sands said. Carrying the package of money under his arm, Sands marched across the parking lot, circled around the building. He walked in the front entrance and through the busy, smoke-filled casino, and took an elevator to the eighteenth floor. At the end of the hallway, he knocked on a door.

Parisi opened the door. He looked both ways in the hallway, allowed Sands to enter. Sands handed him the package.

"No problems?" Parisi said as he tore the package open. He thumbed greenbacks.

"He never knew what hit him," Sands said.

"What was he doing when you went in?"

"He's a fruit. He was fruiting off."

Parisi smiled one of his lewd blue-lipped smiles. "You're the best I've ever seen at this game," he said.

"When will you have Monica out of jail?"

"The bondsman will have her out within two hours," Parisi said. "I'll call you."

"And my money from the phony chips?"

"Come back in two hours and I'll have the money I owe you."

"You're standing there with a hundred grand in a bag and you're telling me to come back for what you owe me?"

"I'd cut off some of this right now, but I'm parlaying a deal in another room right at the moment," Parisi said as he maintained unflinching eye contact. He made a gracious smile. "Go get your wife out of jail and I'll have your money for you."

Outside, Sands found Beadle waiting where he had left him. Together, they walked briskly through the dimly lit parking lot. "Did he come through with the chips money?" Beadle said as they turned this way and that among endless rows of vehicles which, because of the synthetic light, all looked the same color.

"He's still stalling. I can't figure it."

They reached the car Beadle had rented earlier in the day.

"Maybe that sorry-assed Desmond will do a TV talk show about it someday. His new book will be called *The Case of the Cork Soaker's Checkbook.*"

They laughed.

"Thanks for helping me get Monica out," Sands said as they reached the car. "I owe you, old partner."

They reached the car, climbed in. Beadle put his key in the ignition. There was movement in the backseat. Sands whirled.

A man sprang up, pointed a gun. It was Vito. "Turn around and keep your hands where I can see them," he said with an inflection in his voice that meant to Eddie Sands he was ready to kill. It was a tone that every veteran cop comes to recognize for exactly what it is—the promise that death is just a six-pound trigger pull away.

Slowly, Sands turned toward the windshield. He felt his heart pounding, slamming, trying to escape from his chest.

"Drive out of the lot," Vito said to Beadle.

Beadle's eyes moved in Sands's direction.

"What do you want?" Sands said. For some reason, he recalled standing at a doorway in a trailer court off the Boulder highway years ago. He had talked a drunken auto mechanic into giving up a knife he was holding to his wife's throat.

Vito touched the barrel of his gun to the back of Beadle's head. "Drive, motherfucker," he said. "Someone wants to meet you."

"I delivered the money to Tony," Sands said, trying to buy time to size up the situation.

"Start the engine and drive," Vito said. "Or your head comes off."

"Do what he says, Ray," Sands said to the windshield.

A well-dressed couple with arms around each other passed by. The gray artificial light in the parking lot gave their complexions a deathlike pallor. They didn't notice the three sitting in the car. Sands's abdominal muscles were taut, his breathing labored.

Ray Beadle started the engine. He put the car in gear, backed slowly out of the parking space. Just as slowly, he changed gears. He stepped on the accelerator, drove carefully to the exit.

"Turn right."

Beadle complied, pulled into traffic on the crowded Las Vegas Boulevard. They passed the Frontier Hotel.

"Where are we going?" Sands said.

"Everything will be okay if you do what I say."

"You've got a lot of balls taking us without any help," Sands said.

"Shut the fuck up."

Beadle steered past the Hacienda Hotel, some service stations, and a small business district at the north end of the Strip. In front of them was nothing but darkness and desert.

"Who wants to talk to us out in the desert?" Sands said.

Vito said nothing.

Eddie Sands made a circular motion with his left

hand and prayed that Beadle would notice. "Looks like we're gonna get killed, Ray," Sands said as they left behind the lights of Las Vegas. Beadle blinked rapidly to show that he understood. The car accelerated steadily.

"You gonna bury us?" Beadle said to Vito with his voice cracking. The car accelerated.

"You're going too fast. Slow down," Vito said. He sounded worried.

For a moment, Sands thought of Monica. He imagined her head resting on his shoulder, her hand clasping his. He smelled her hair. Then he allowed his legs and arms to become taut, ready. Suddenly he whirled, lunged at Vito. With a catlike motion he snatched the barrel of the .22, twisted. The gun fired. With the immediate ear-splitting crack of the revolver, Beadle shrieked. The car swerved.

Eddie Sands was still gripping the gun with both hands as he fought for control, for his life. There was the sound of wheels hitting rocks and gravel as the car left the road. Suddenly Sands felt the world turning upside down. He continued to struggle for the weapon. It fired twice more. Glass shattered. Finally the car ground to a stop on its side. Thrown together in the wreck, Sands and Vito were face to face, so close that Sands could smell the other man's sour breath. The gun was still between them. Sands managed to get a grip on Vito's thumb. Slowly, as Vito made little groans, Sands pried the thumb away from the butt of the revolver. He shoved downward on it with all the adrenaline strength he could muster. As he continued to force the thumb backward, Vito emitted a long, controlled moan. Finally, with a powerful life-or-death effort, Sands forced the thumb fully backward. There was a sound like a green twig breaking. Vito's moan changed to a deafening, full male scream.

Sands yanked the gun away.

He worked the trigger until the gun was empty. Vito screamed as the bullets hit him. His body twisted, convulsed, and his head slammed loudly against a window. Finally, he stopped moving and there was a long, wet gasp as the last air he would ever emit came from his lungs. His body went slack.

The interior of the upturned car was filled with the smell of gunsmoke and blood.

Eddie Sands disentangled himself, reached for Beadle, who was lying slumped beneath him. He slid his hand under Beadle's collar, touched his carotid artery. Nothing. "Ray. Ray," he said. Then saw the hole in the back of Beadle's head. "No. Oh, God, no," he said.

Sands found himself scrambling, crawling upward and out of the passenger window of the wrecked sedan as if death would take him too if he lingered. He dropped into sagebrush, backed away from the wreckage.

The desert was still, and for as far as he could see there was dark gray landscape broken only by a string of telephone poles and wires wetted with moonlight. Regaining control of himself, he checked to see if he was injured. Nothing but a few scrapes. He hurried up an embankment to the roadway.

For a moment, he just stood there hyperventilating, sick with fear, as he ran through the details of what happened. There were headlights in the distance, and he suddenly realized he was still holding the gun in his hand. He hurried back down the embankment, waited as he heard the sound of the car coming closer. Finally, the car sped by. He looked about. The wrecked sedan had ended up lower than road level in the sagebrush, hidden from view of those passing on the highway, at least until morning.

His mind raced. He forced himself to return to the wreckage, climbed back inside. With some difficulty, he removed Beadle's gun holster and badge. He shoved them in a side pocket of his suit jacket. He used a handkerchief to wipe his fingerprints from the barrel and trigger guard of Vito's gun, then dropped it near his hand. He climbed back out of the wreckage.

He told himself that there was nothing to tie him to

the wreck and the bodies. Beadle had rented the car under his own name. He started to run toward Las Vegas, stopped himself, slowed down to a deliberate pace. It took him two hours to make his way back, keeping out of sight of cars and trucks passing on the highway. Finally, he reached the edge of the Strip.

From a service station, he called a taxi. On the trip back to Monica's apartment to pick up his car he told an amused driver that he'd had a fight with his wife about losing his paycheck at the crap table and that she had taken the car and headed back to L.A.

He was lucky at the city jail—the cop on duty remembered him and opened up the visiting room of the women's section. As Monica sat down on the bench opposite him on the other side of the glass partition, Sands thought she looked ill.

"How did it go?" she said.

"Ray's dead."

"Jesus. What happened?"

"I took the money to Parisi. Then he tried to hit me," Sands said, his voice cracking. "Ray got shot."

"Why would Parisi try to hit you if you already gave him his money?"

"Somebody must have put some paper on me."

"But who...?"

"Doesn't really matter. The point is, Parisi has paper on me and I'm dead, hon."

"What about my bail?"

"Parisi's got the hundred grand. I would never be able to come up with enough collateral without him."

Monica lowered her head. After a moment, she looked up. There were tears in her eyes. "Poor Ray," she said.

"I'm gonna have to do it, hon," Sands said.

"You mean..."

"I'm gonna have to deal with the feds."

"If you take the stand, things will never be the same. Your name will be shit."

"It's the only way to get you out."

"You don't have to do this for me. With good time and all, I'll probably end up doing less than two years." She swallowed hard. "It's not that long."

Sands felt the taste of tears in his throat. "I'm no good without you," he said.

"Oh, Eddie, I'm so afraid."

"I am too, hon. But there's no other way."

She sobbed. He reached out to comfort her and touched glass.

"I know you really love me, baby," she cried. "You would never do this if you didn't love me."

At a pay phone just outside the visiting room, Eddie Sands thumbed through a soiled telephone book, found the number for the FBI. He dialed, asked to speak with Agent Novak. An operator asked his name and the number of the phone he was calling from. As Eddie Sands gave the information to her, he realized he was shaking so badly he could hardly hold the phone receiver. The operator told him Novak would call him back in a few minutes.

As Eddie Sands set the receiver back on the hook, he surveyed the graffiti scrawled on the wall near the phone. "Fuck Apartheid." "Chuey eats it." A few names and phone numbers, attorneys and bail bondsmen. Above the instrument itself, written in backhand script, was a message: "Leroy Stane is the rat who put my man inside." Eddie Sands wondered whether he should call Leroy Stane, whoever the fuck he was, and ask him what it was like to be a snitch.

The phone rang. Sands let it ring three times before he picked up the receiver. It was Novak.

"We need to talk," Sands said.

"About what?"

"About what you want from me."

"Can you come to the office?"

"No."

"Then meet me at the Mobil service station at the end of the Strip," Novak said. "The one with the big signboard. I'll be parked in back."

29 Eddie Sands cruised into the driveway entrance of the service station. The lights in the station were off, but from above, an enormous illuminated billboard, depicting a dripping bikini-clad blonde lounging next to the Tropicana swimming pool, bathed the lot in weak gray light. He pulled past the gas pumps.

Novak's car was parked behind the station. Sands parked next to it, turned off the engine. He climbed out, looked about, wandered to the front. Novak was not there. He headed back toward his car. As he passed the corner of the station building he heard a noise like a door creaking.

The barrel of a gun touched his neck.

"Easy, Eddie," Novak said.

Sands stood still as he was frisked. "Clean," Haynes said.

Novak stepped in front of Sands. "Nothing personal," Novak said. He shoved his revolver back into a holster. He was wearing a sport coat and an open-collar shirt.

"It's just that our doctor recommends that we shouldn't allow bullets to enter our bodies," Haynes said.

"Don't get the idea that I came here to bend over for you feds," Eddie Sands said.

Novak reached into the side pocket of his sport coat, took out a pack of cigarettes. He offered one to Sands. Sands accepted. Novak flamed a lighter, moved the light close to the end of Sands's cigarette. Sands puffed. Then Novak lit his own.

"I'm willing to do something for you people, but I want some guarantees," Sands said.

"Like what?"

"I want Monica released, out of jail, and all charges on her dropped immediately."

"In exchange for what?"

"In exchange for Parisi's head." He took a deep drag on the cigarette, blew smoke.

"What does that mean?"

"It means I can tell you how he runs the casino skim operation, how his organization is run, where his juice comes from. The works."

Novak sauntered to his car, leaned on the fender. "Are you offering to testify against him in front of a federal grand jury?"

"I don't want to testify."

Novak puffed smoke. "The only way I can put Parisi away is with an indictment. To get an indictment someone has to testify."

"People know me in this town."

"I know it's not an easy decision," Novak said.

Sands realized his hands were sweating.

"I'm offering to give you enough information to put him in the joint. I just don't want to do it on a witness stand . . . on front street."

"Front street is where all the big cases are made."

"So you're telling me that if I won't go before a grand jury then there's no deal?"

"That's right. Monica will have to take the fall."

"I know what you're doing," Sands said. "I know your fucking game."

"The decision is yours," Novak said. With a roar, a trailer truck sped past the service station.

"What I want is my wife out of jail."

"What I want is you before a federal grand jury. Without that we can't do business."

"Let's say I agree to the grand-jury bit," Sands said. "Would you let Monica out?"

"I could get the bail lowered. She'd be released on her own recognizance."

"I want the charges dropped completely."

"As soon as your grand-jury testimony was completed, all charges on her would be dropped," Novak said.

"If I testify, I want immunity from prosecution on anything I testify about."

"Sounds fair enough."

"And I want a new identity for Monica and me. We want to be placed in the witness protection program."

"That can be arranged," Novak said.

"Then we have a deal?"

John Novak took one last puff on his cigarette, dropped it, crushed it with his heel. He looked Eddie Sands in the eye. "We have a deal," Novak said. "Do you know where the Wheel of Fortune Motel is?"

Sands nodded.

"Go straight there. Rent two rooms. Register one under the name Novak, the other under a phony name. Wait there for me."

Sands headed toward his car, climbed in.

"Do you think Elliot will go for the deal you just made?" Haynes said.

Novak just stood there in thought for a moment. "I'm not sure Elliot actually wants anyone to take the stand against Parisi."

Haynes stepped closer. "Are you saying what I think

you're saying?" he said in a somber tone.

Novak looked his partner directly in the eye.

"Elliot's no dummy," Haynes said. "If you're right, you'd never be able to prove it. Not in a million years."

"It might be worth a try," Novak said.

"You're serious about this."

"You don't have to help. It's strictly up to you."

"You can count me in *one hundred and fifty percent*," Haynes said with his best Elliot smile.

"We're gonna have to move fast, Red."

About twenty minutes later, John Novak stood alone at the telephone booth at the corner of the service station's lot. He dropped change, dialed a number. The phone rang.

Elliot answered. He sounded fully awake.

"This is Novak. Sorry to bother you so late, but we need to talk. Eddie Sands has turned. He's ready to testify against Parisi."

"Where are you?"

Novak told him. Elliot said he'd be right there.

Less than twenty minutes later, Elliot drove into the service station and parked his station wagon next to a gas pump. Novak moved to the vehicle, opened the door, climbed in.

Elliot turned off the engine.

"How did you get Sands to turn?"

"I promised to drop charges on his wife and give him immunity."

"I love it."

"And put him in the witness protection program."

"No problem whatsoever."

"When do you recommend we put him in front of a grand jury?" Novak said.

"If we get into a big rush and throw him in front of a grand jury before we have a case ready, it could hurt us in the long run."

"Until we have him on the stand there's no way to lock in his testimony."

"I'm not sure when the next grand jury will—"

"I checked," Novak interrupted. "The grand jury is scheduled to meet at eleven a.m."

"Of course," Elliot said. He studied Novak for a moment, then gave his key ring a little twirl.

"Sands will be a better witness than Bruno could ever have been," Novak said. "Parisi got him out of the joint. He was on Parisi's payroll when he was a cop. He can sink the ship."

"I understand how anxious you are to get him on the stand, but my best advice is to proceed carefully. A series of appearances before the grand jury—"

"I just got off the phone with the Bureau agent-in-charge," Novak lied. "He agrees with me that the grand jury as soon as possible is the best way to go."

"And if I disagree?"

"He's willing to phone D.C. and wake people up, let them decide."

"No need for a Bureau–Strike Force squabble. I'm behind you a hundred and fifty percent. If you feel that strongly, we'll put Sands on the stand immediately."

Novak unlocked the car door. "I'll have him debriefed fully by eleven a.m.," he said.

"Considering the circumstances, it's probably better to put him on the stand cold."

"You don't want me to debrief?"

"If he's our ticket to putting Parisi away, then let's not give the defense the opportunity to say we coached his testimony."

"Not even—"

"I feel strongly that the best way to go is to put him on the stand cold. Keep him on ice. Don't let him speak to anyone before eleven."

Novak shrugged. "If you think that's what we should do," Novak said.

Elliot gave him a friendly cuff on the shoulder. "By the way, congratulations on turning the most important witness in the history of the Las Vegas Strike Force. I mean that."

"Thanks," Novak said. He opened the door and climbed out of the station wagon. His mind raced.

"One more thing," Elliot said.

Calmly, Novak turned, leaned down to the open passenger window.

"I'll take care of the paperwork to get formal witness protection authorized, but in the meantime it's best if you stay with him personally. If he starts to get cold feet, you can hold his hand."

Novak nodded. "Sure."

"I think it's best to stay away from the federal courthouse. Someone might see him."

"I'll take him to a motel."

"As soon as you get a room I want you to call me."

"Sure."

Elliot looked as if he wanted to say something else. He started the engine. "One more itty-bitty thing," he said, raising his voice to be heard over the sound of the engine. "I didn't get a chance to tell you today, but I was able to quash the suggestion from D.C. that you and Haynes be pulled off the case."

"Thanks," Novak said, though he felt like grabbing Elliot and pulling him through the window. Elliot gave a little salute, drove out of the service station.

Novak stood there in thought as Elliot's car moved down the highway. The station wagon's taillights faded into the distance and finally disappeared.

Novak's attention turned to the parking lot of the auto-parts store down the street. Vehicle headlights came on, and Haynes steered out of the darkened parking lot onto the highway. He cruised directly to the service station, squealed brakes as he came to a halt. Novak met him as he climbed out of the driver's door.

"He left his house about three minutes after you phoned him," Haynes said. "I followed him from his house to a convenience market." Haynes reached into his shirt pocket, removed a small notebook. "A market at 85463 Boulder Highway. He parked, made a call from a pay phone—a short call—then he headed straight here. I stayed way back. He never made the tail."

"How far was the telephone booth from his place?" Novak said.

"Four, maybe five blocks—right after you come out of the residential area onto the highway. At first I thought he was going to meet someone, but he just made a quick call."

"Right to Tony Parisi."

"I hope you're right."

"I want you to stop by Metro PD," Novak said. "Borrow three of their walkie-talkies, a mouthpiece transmitter, a couple of shotguns, and a box of shells. Don't go to the office. And talk to no one."

"I get it."

"We need another man. Roll out Frank Tyde. Don't call him. Pick him up at home. Head for Judge Traynor's house."

"Judge Traynor's house?"

"She'll be expecting you," Novak said.

 **30** The Wheel of Fortune Motel, like a lot of the motels which existed solely because of their proximity to the downtown Las Vegas casinos, had seen better days. The balconies of the three-story rectangular structure looked out at slow-moving glitter-gulch traffic, an undersized swimming pool surrounded by a chain-link fence, and a sprinkling of old cars in the parking lot, but the rates were afford-able to down-on-their-luck gamblers and FBI agents try-ing to keep within the limits of their expense allowance.

Novak parked his car near the registration office where it could be easily spotted from the street. He checked his wristwatch. It was one in the morning. He made his way to Room 27, knocked on the door.

Eddie Sands let him in. Novak immediately locked the door behind him, then checked the door to the ad-joining room to make sure it was unlocked. Sands, wearing socks without shoes, returned to a small sofa.

Novak moved to an end table, picked up the phone receiver. He dialed. As the phone rang, Novak noticed that the television was tuned to a talk show. A man who had won an egg-eating contest was being interviewed by the gray-haired host. Elliot answered. "Novak here. I've got Sands at the Wheel of Fortune Motel, Room 27."

"Thanks for keeping me informed. Everything okay?"

"Fine."

"Try to get some sleep," Elliot said. "I'll see you in the grand-jury room." The phone clicked.

Novak set the receiver down.

"Who was that?" Sands said.

"The attorney-in-charge of the Organized Crime Strike Force."

"Secrets don't last very long in Las Vegas."

"Does Tony have anyone in law enforcement on his payroll now?" Novak said as he moved to the front door, fastened the deal-bolt lock, then the chain.

"He got me out of Terminal Island by funneling juice to the Federal Parole Board."

"Other than that." Novak tugged at a corner of the curtain to close it fully.

Eddie Sands shrugged. "He once mentioned if anything was happening he would get a call. But he would have no reason to give me a name. He would never tell anyone."

Novak flipped the light switch off. He tugged the curtain back an inch or so, kept his eye on the lot. "What did Parisi say about Bruno Santoro getting blown up?" Novak said as he continued to stare out the window.

"He said Bruno was ready to testify against him, so he had him clipped."

"What were his exact words?"

"Something like 'Bruno was going to sing a song for the feds. So I made him disappear.' Then he said something about a bomb. Then he laughed. That was about it."

Novak opened a dresser drawer, removed some stationery, made a note of what Sands had said. He lit a cigarette, grabbed a chair, and set it next to the window. He straddled the chair.

"What are you worried about?"

"Nothing."

"If you weren't worried you wouldn't be staring out the window."

Sands moved to the dresser, removed a can from a six-pack of beer, popped the top. He offered it to Novak. Novak accepted.

"Who wired Bruno's car?" Novak asked.

"Probably the Corcoran brothers."

"The dudes who hang out at the Golden Gate Sports Book?"

"None other."

"They know bombs?" Novak said.

"Tony paid their way to a survival school. The contract went from Tony to Vito to them."

Sands sat down. Both men sipped beer. "How did they know where Bruno's car was located in order to plant the bomb?" Novak said. "Did someone follow him?"

Sands shrugged. "He got a call. He told me he got a call from someone who knew Bruno was a snitch."

Sands stood up slowly. "That's why you're keeping all the lights off in here...because there's a leak in your department."

Novak didn't answer. He kept an eye on the parking lot.

"Eddie, I want you to tell me everything you know about Tony Parisi. From the first day you met."

Sands took a big pull from the beer, sat down again. He began to speak.

About an hour later he was still talking. Novak had used up almost five sheets of motel stationery making notes. As he had done intermittently, he tugged the curtain back an inch or two, peeked out. A black Cadillac pulled into the parking lot, cruised along the rows of parked vehicles, then drove out of the lot and across the street. Two men climbed out. They looked about, moved to the trunk, opened it, lifted something out, shut the trunk.

Sands stopped talking. "What is it?"

As the two men moved under a streetlight on their way to the motel, Novak got a better look. They were black and wore business suits. Novak stood up, pulled his gun.

Sands moved to the window, peeked out. "The Corcoran brothers."

Novak pointed to the adjoining room. Sands picked up his shoes, moved quickly.

There was the sound of approaching footsteps. Two silhouettes moved slowly past the window to the door, stopped.

Novak backed away from the window, followed Sands into the adjoining room. He gently pulled the door to the room closed, turned the latch. He stood in darkness.

They heard the sounds of a pump shotgun chambering a round, of the door being kicked, splintering, and of people rushing into the room, moving about quickly. Novak positioned himself next to the connecting door. He pointed his revolver at the door, at chest level, prepared to fire at whoever entered. He could hear Sands breathing heavily.

"Muthafuckas have gone," said one of the men in the other room. Footsteps approached the adjoining door. The doorknob turned. Novak's trigger finger tightened. He felt a warm survival rush at his temples that reminded him of Vietnam.

Then he heard footsteps running out of the room and down along the balcony.

Novak vaulted to the window, pulled back the blind about an inch. Sands joined him. They watched as the gunmen ran across the street, jumped into the Cadillac, and sped away.

Novak stepped away from the window. He said nothing.

"You should have let 'em have it," Sands said.

"They'll come back for me. Why didn't you kill 'em?"

Novak moved to the door. He opened it, looked about. Because of the commotion, people were coming out of rooms. He and Sands went to his G-car and climbed in.

No lights were visible at Lorraine Traynor's house when Novak cruised past. At the corner, he turned right. He spotted Haynes's car, pulled to the curb, and turned off the engine. He and Sands got out. In the darkness, they walked down the sidewalk to an empty lot which faced the rear of Lorraine Traynor's house.

"Where are we going?" Sands said as Novak trudged across the empty lot. Novak touched an index finger to his lips. "Sssshhh." Sands shrugged.

They climbed over a fence, crossed the backyard, and entered through the rear door of the house. Lorraine Traynor, Haynes, and Frank Tyde were sitting at a dining table which was littered with city maps, affidavit forms, coffee cups. Two Remington pump shotguns rested against the wall.

"Good morning, judge," Novak said. He introduced Eddie Sands.

"Please sit down," she said. She left her seat, moved to a dining cart, poured coffee into cups.

Frank Tyde tapped his palm over his mouth as he yawned. "I hope we're getting overtime for this," he said. Haynes gave him a dirty look.

Lorraine Traynor served coffee to Sands, then Novak. "What happened?" she said.

"We had visitors," Novak said. "The Corcoran brothers, carrying heavy iron. We watched them from the next room."

"I'll be damned," Haynes said.

Lorraine Traynor sat down at the table. She tapped her fingers on her lower lip for a moment. "Mr. Sands, I'm ordering that you be provided protection as a federal witness. You will remain here in my home until further notice. Agent Tyde, you will remain with Mr. Sands. Why don't you two go in the kitchen and make yourselves something to eat?"

Tyde slapped his stomach. "Sounds good to me." Sands followed him out of the room. Lorraine Traynor picked up a pen, made a note on a legal pad, turned to Novak. "What did Sands have to say?"

Novak took out his notes, perused them for a moment. "Parisi told him he got the word from a snitch that Bruno Santoro was going to be at the Highland Coffee Shop."

Lorraine Traynor made a note on the pad. "That doesn't do us a lot of good in tying Parisi to the murder," she said. "We need something solid against him. A piece of evidence that is, on its face, undeniable."

"Sands thinks the bombing was done by the Corcoran brothers," Novak said. "They have the training."

"Let's arrest 'em. I'll crack their heads together to make 'em talk," Haynes said.

Lorraine Traynor looked askance at Haynes. Haynes gave her a little smile. She turned to Novak. "If you think it's the way to go I'll authorize the arrest of the Corcoran brothers."

Novak stood up, leaned against the wall. "The Corcorans are solid cons. Chances are they'll never talk. And if they did it would be Parisi's word against theirs."

"Does that mean that you want to interview Parisi first and try to get him to incriminate himself?" she said.

Novak shook his head. "That would be a waste of time. He's never given a statement to the police in his life."

"Let's just arrest him," Haynes said. "If he thinks we have a case he might talk."

Novak sipped coffee. "It won't work," he said.

Lorraine Traynor sat back in her chair. "It sounds to me like you have something else in mind."

"I do. It's a long shot."

"I'm listening," she said.

"Elliot, Red, and I were the only ones who knew Bruno was going to be at the coffee shop that day," Novak said.

She made another note. "The fact that a secret got out isn't evidence of anything. It's possible Parisi had Bruno followed to the coffee shop. Any number of scenarios could—" Suddenly Lorraine Traynor stopped speaking as she realized what Novak was getting at.

"If you are going to do that I'll have to call the Attorney General," she said.

31

It was almost two in the morning.

As Novak cruised slowly along the well-lit street looking for Elliot's address, he went over the details of the plan in his mind.

He slowed down. The houses were two-story stucco jobs, all with driveways big enough to accommodate three cars and a boat. It was one of the most expensive residential areas in Las Vegas. Novak spotted the house number he was looking for. He pulled into the driveway, climbed out of the car. There were lights on inside the house.

At the door, Novak rang the bell. A minute or two later, he heard footsteps inside. They stopped on the other side of the door. "Who's there?" Elliot said.

"Novak."

At least thirty seconds passed before anything happened. Then Elliot unlocked the door and opened it. He was dressed in pajamas and robe.

"I've been trying to phone you at the Wheel of Fortune," Elliot said. "Where the hell have you been?"

"The manager there was asking a lot of questions, so I checked out."

"Why the hell didn't you call me?"

"I didn't want to talk on the phone."

Elliot opened the door fully. "Come in."

Novak stepped in, followed Elliot across a large, tastefully decorated living room and into a kitchen that might have been featured in a Sunday supplement. "I know you wouldn't be here unless it was something important."

"Is there anyone else here?" Novak said.

"We're alone."

"Sands is talking."

"I told you I don't want him talking before he gets on the witness stand."

"He's shook up," Novak said. "I can't help it if he has diarrhea of the mouth."

Elliot stood there for a moment as if in pain, then regained composure. He turned the heat on under a coffee pot.

"His usefulness as a witness could be blown if he makes a bunch of dumb statements ahead of time."

"I can't keep him quiet. He's on the edge."

"Snitch's remorse. Understandable."

"It's more than that," Novak said. "He doesn't trust us."

Elliot turned to face him. "How so?"

"Sands says we have a leak at the Strike Force. Specifically, that's how Bruno Santoro was fingered."

Elliot filled two cups, came to the table, sat down. "A leak," he said.

"He says that someone is funneling information to Tony Parisi...that it's common knowledge he has an insider on his payroll."

"All hoods brag about having a cop or a prosecutor on the payroll. It's invariably bullshit."

"What the man is telling me fits with what has been happening at the Strike Force."

"What evidence does he have? Let's talk some hard fucking facts."

"Only the people in our office knew Bruno was an informant."

"Does Sands have any clue to the identity of the leak? Anything of evidentiary value whatsoever?"

Novak shook his head.

"Eddie Sands is just trying to build up his value as a witness," Elliot said.

"He's already committed to take the stand," Novak said. "He gains nothing by lying to us."

"Sometimes snitches lie just to lie."

"Sands was a cop. I believe him."

"You're a hundred and fifty percent right," Elliot said. "We have to take this seriously."

Novak nodded. "I'll have Sands at the grand jury at eleven a.m.," he said. He finished his coffee and stood up.

They walked to the door. Elliot stuck out his hand, shook with Novak. "This is going to be the biggest organized-crime indictment in the country, John. And I am personally going to see that you are promoted."

"Thanks," Novak said. Though it was difficult, he looked Elliot directly in the eye.

"Which motel?"

"Pardon?"

"The motel where you have Sands."

"The Algiers, Room 302," Novak said.

"Who is with him at this moment?"

"No one."

"Isn't that kind of dangerous?"

"He's not going anywhere as long as we have his wife."

"We have to keep his location on a *need-to-know* basis . . . one hundred and fifty percent *need-to-know*," Elliot said. "I don't want anyone except you and me to know where you have him stashed."

Outside, Novak climbed into his sedan and sped onto

Boulder Highway. He turned right and continued at a high rate of speed until he reached the first commercial area. It was an all-night convenience market with a small parking lot. There were three cars parked in the lot: a Volkswagen, an old Chevy, and Lorraine Traynor's Dodge van. He slowed down, flicked his headlights on and off a couple of times as he drove past. The headlights on the van did the same.

It took him less than ten minutes to get to the Algiers Motel, a hundred-room two-story place built around a circular swimming pool. He parked down the street and hurried to the motel. Room 302 was on the second floor at the end of the walkway. He climbed steps, knocked on the door. The door was opened by Red Haynes. Novak stepped inside. "The bait is out," he said as Haynes closed the door behind him.

The room was decorated with fuchsia wallpaper and mirrors. Lying on the bed were two pump-action shotguns. He moved to the curtain, peeked out. There was no one in the parking lot. He picked up a shotgun.

"Three in the magazine and one in the chamber...all double-O buck," Haynes said. "How do you want to do this?"

Novak surveyed the room quickly. He grabbed chairs from a table, placed them in the corners of the room facing the door. "I think we should let 'em come in," he said. "Maintain your firing position."

"Gotcha," Haynes said. He picked up the other shotgun, moved to one of the chairs, sat down.

Novak moved about the room flicking off light switches. In semidarkness, he went to the other chair, sat down, rested the shotgun on his lap. The only light in the room was a faint gray illumination coming through the curtains. There was the barely audible sound of police calls coming from the walkie-talkie on the floor next to Haynes.

Leaning back in the chair, Novak relived his last conversation with Bruno Santoro. He wondered how many times his mind had gone over the scene. He thought of Lorraine, and then, God knew why, he remembered being on the bus leaving the army induction center in Philadelphia. Sitting in a window seat on the crowded bus, he waved goodbye to his father and uncle—strapping, red-faced Slavs who had taken the afternoon off at the Hardesty Steel Mill to see him off. Standing on the sidewalk, tears streaming down their faces, they waved until the bus was out of sight.

"What if they just walk up here and toss a hand grenade through the window?" Haynes said. "These guys are bombers."

"They'll come in. They're gonna want to make sure they're getting Sands."

Resting his shotgun on his shoulder like a duck hunter, Novak moved to the window, pulled the curtain back a few inches, peeked out. He returned to his seat.

"This could get real nasty," Haynes said a few minutes later.

"How are your sons doing?" Novak said to break the tension in the room.

"Football and screaming rock music, that's all they live for. I call it jock and roll.... Maybe Elliot won't tip off Parisi. Maybe there's some other explanation."

"I don't think so."

Haynes cleared his throat. "We could be sitting here for nothing," he said. "Maybe Parisi found out some other way. Maybe Frank Tyde is rotten."

"Red Haynes, the eternal optimist," Novak said. Nothing was said for a long time. Novak checked his watch. They had been in the room almost two hours.

"The sun's gonna come up pretty soon. They won't do anything then."

"Never know."

"How long we gonna sit here?" Haynes said finally.

"I don't know."

There was the sound of footsteps on the stairs outside. Novak moved to the curtain, peeked out. The Corcoran brothers were moving up the steps toward the room. "The Corcorans. This is it, Red." Novak moved back to the corner of the room.

Red Haynes picked up the walkie-talkie, pressed the transmit button. "Federal officers need help," he whispered. "Algiers Motel...Room 302." He turned down the volume.

Novak lifted his shotgun, aimed it at the door. Haynes did the same.

There was knocking at the door.

"Who's there?" Novak said.

"Police. Is that you, Novak?"

"Yes."

The sound of shuffling directly outside the door, whispering, then a terrific crack as the door was kicked in.

As the Corcoran brothers raced into the room with sawed-off shotguns, Novak and Haynes fired simultaneously. The room exploded in shotgun flame and smoke. One intruder spun backward and was hurtled through the doorway. Glass shattered as the other was flung against the bay window. Novak fired again and blew him through the window and onto the walkway.

Holding the smoking shotgun at the ready, Novak moved to the light switch, flicked it on. At the doorway, he stepped across a body as Haynes grabbed the sawed-off shotgun from the floor. Novak moved cautiously out the door. The other man was lying facedown on the walkway. He was twitching. There was the sound of sirens.

Haynes followed him outside, carrying the walkie-talkie. He was breathing hard. "Federal officers requesting an ambulance to the Algiers Motel," he said. "Shots fired. Man down."

"Ten four," replied the dispatcher.

"You all right?" Novak said to Haynes.

Haynes nodded. "It's Elliot. He's working for Parisi. The dirty son of a bitch."

"I want you to stay here and handle the scene," Novak said. "Wait fifteen minutes and call Elliot. Tell him what happened."

"Good luck," Haynes said.

• • •

Novak left the Algiers Motel and drove down the Strip to Boulder Highway. Lorraine Traynor's van was still parked in the parking lot of the convenience store. Novak drove past and parked his car at the rear of a supermarket so that it was shielded from the street. He locked his car and hurried back to the convenience-store parking lot. Lorraine slid open the door of her van. He climbed in. They embraced. Novak checked his wristwatch. "Haynes should be calling Elliot right about now."

"I hope you're right," she said.

"Elliot has to call Parisi. He can't just sit there at home."

"My fingers are crossed," Lorraine said.

Neither spoke for a while. There was only the intermittent sound of cars and trucks gusting by on the highway and distant bluegrass music coming from a radio in the supermarket.

About five minutes later, Elliot drove into the lot, parked near the pay telephone. He stepped out of his car. He was wearing a pajama top over his trousers. He looked about carefully, as if to check the automobiles parked in the lot, then sauntered to the pay phone. Novak reached to the floorboard and flicked on a portable high-frequency receiver/tape recorder. From the instrument came the sound of a telephone ringing. Then a click.

"Stardust Hotel," an operator said.

Elliot cleared his throat. "Room 8577," he said.

The phone clicked twice, then rang. Tony Parisi said hello.

"You fucked up," Elliot said.

"Where are you calling from?" Parisi said.

"A pay phone. Where do you think I'm calling from?"

"What do you mean I fucked up?"

"Your people are dead. They went to the Algiers and got themselves blown up by the FBI."

"What about Sands?"

"Alive. And scheduled to sit in front of a grand jury at eleven a.m."

"This is what happens when people get in a big fuckin' hurry," Tony Parisi said. "Who told you?"

"An FBI agent named Haynes called me. He and Novak wasted the two dummies you sent there. Do you understand what this means? Sands is going to *sing*. You are down the toilet if Sands sits down on the fucking witness stand."

"No, *you* are down the toilet if you don't fix all of this. That's what I pay you for."

"There is only so much I can do at this point," Elliot said.

"Postpone the grand jury. Stall the case."

"They'll know."

"What matters isn't what they *know*. It's what they can *prove*. Isn't that right, Mr. *Strike Force Attorney?*"

"I'll do what I can," Elliot said. "But this can't go on forever."

"Get this. If I get indicted, you go to sleep with the fishes. You go to the fucking cemetery."

There was a click. Elliot rested the phone on the hook.

Novak turned off the recorder.

"That ought to do it," Lorraine Traynor said.

John Novak flung open the side door, stepped out of the van.

Elliot stopped abruptly. He looked as if he had suddenly lost his breath. He stared as Novak walked past him to the pay phone, picked up the receiver, unscrewed the mouthpiece, dropped the transmitter into his hand. He held it up for Elliot to see. "You're under arrest for obstruction of justice and conspiracy to murder Bruno Santoro," he said.

Elliot had no color in his face. "You don't have a court order to bug that phone."

Judge Lorraine Traynor stepped out of the van. "Yes, he does," she said. "I'm the United States district judge who signed it. Be advised that you have the right to remain silent and that anything you say can and will be used against you. You have the right to speak to an attorney and to have the attorney present during questioning. If you so desire and cannot afford one, an attorney will be appointed for you without charge before questioning. Do you understand each of these rights I have explained to you?"

The dazed Elliot nodded.

"Do you wish to give up the right to remain silent?" Lorraine Traynor said.

Elliot stared at the highway.

"Before you say no," she said, "perhaps you'd like to know that the Attorney General of the United States is aware of this situation, and that I will be the one who sets your bail."

"The tape is loud and clear," Novak said. "You're slam-dunk."

After a while Elliot's lips moved as to speak. "Yes," he said under his breath.

"Do you wish to give up the right to an attorney and to have him with you during questioning?"

"Yes."

"You'll have to speak up."

"Yes."

**32** It was chilly in the parking lot. Elliot leaned against the side of Lorraine's van. His hands covered his face for a moment, then he stared at the highway, which suddenly was deserted.

Novak noticed that Lorraine looked cold. He offered his jacket. She accepted.

"You know what you have to do," Novak said.

Elliot continued to stare at the highway.

"You want me to testify against Tony."

"That's right."

Elliot shook his head. "Not if I have to do time. If I have to go to prison, I'm not going to cooperate." Elliot spoke without looking at Novak.

Lorraine blew into her right, then her left hand. She crossed her arms across her chest and squeezed. "The Department of Justice would never approve a deal for no time. And if such a deal was made, no federal judge would abide by it. You're going to have to do some time."

"Time can be broken down," Elliot said.

"Make an offer," Novak said.

For a moment, Elliot just stood there staring at the highway. Finally, his mouth opened as if to speak, but nothing came out.

"How do I know that either of you is authorized to make a deal with me?"

"Would you like to call the Attorney General and ask him that?" Lorraine said. "I have his home phone number."

Elliot touched his fingertips to his lips. "I don't feel well."

"In another few minutes, there won't be enough time to do what we need to do," Novak said.

Elliot let out his breath. "I'll plead guilty if I can be guaranteed probation."

"No deal," Novak said.

"I'll do two months custody and the rest probation," Elliot said after staring for a while.

"You're not being realistic," Lorraine Traynor said.

"I can fight this case."

Novak took out a package of cigarettes, tapped on it. "You're an experienced prosecutor. How many cases do you know of where the defendant beat wiretap evidence? The jury will hear you talking shit with Parisi." He hung a cigarette on his lip, struck a match, puffed smoke. "Juries don't like to hear defendants talk like that."

"This whole thing isn't what it seems to be," Elliot said weakly. His head moved slowly from side to side. "If I'm going to risk everything to turn in Parisi there is no reason I should have to serve more than six months custody."

Lorraine Traynor rubbed her hands together. "The lowest the Attorney General will approve is eight years —two years custody and the rest of the sentence broken down to probation and community service. You'll be disbarred, but with good time you would be inside no longer than eighteen months."

Elliot slid his hands into his pockets. His eyes were full. "I'm not going to risk my life testifying against Tony and then go to jail for two years besides."

Novak moved closer to him. "Your family will be sitting in the courtroom. They'll hear the tape," he said. "Reporters will be parked in front of your house."

"And two years will just be the beginning," Lorraine said. "The Department of Justice will want to make an example out of you."

Elliot wiped an eye, looked at his hand. "I don't want to be fingerprinted."

"I order that you not be fingerprinted or booked," Judge Traynor said. "And that you appear before the federal grand jury at eleven a.m. to testify."

Elliot nodded. Lorraine Traynor returned to her van, climbed in. Elliot turned to Novak. Novak turned, walked away.

Driving along the Las Vegas Strip, Novak passed the Algiers Motel, where the parking lot was cluttered with police cars and ambulances, all with blinking emergency lights. He swerved into the circular driveway of the Stardust Hotel and parked at the curb near the front door. He brushed past a doorman, entered.

At the eighth floor, he stepped off an elevator and sauntered down the hallway. At Room 8577, he knocked on the door. There was the sound of footsteps. He took out his badge and held it up to the peephole. The lock clicked. Then the door opened. Parisi was wearing a blue terry-cloth bathrobe.

"I just want to talk to you for a minute."

"I'm sleeping. Come back later." He shut the door.

"I just arrested Elliot," Novak said in a loud voice.

The door opened again. "Who's he?" Parisi said.

"Mind if I step in for a moment?"

Parisi flipped a light switch on, turned around, and

headed into the apartment. Novak stepped inside, closed the door behind him.

"I'll listen to you, but I'm not making any statement," Parisi said as he stepped to the bar. He ran water into a glass, took a drink, spit into the sink.

Novak moved to the middle of the room. "Elliot has agreed to testify against you."

"I don't know what the fuck you're talking about."

"What I'm talking about is a trip to the joint," Novak said.

"So you're here to arrest me?"

"Actually, I just wanted to get together with you before things started to get out of control," Novak said.

"What is that supposed to mean?"

"I'm here to explore all the avenues with you...so to speak."

Parisi's worried look changed to a nervous grin. "If you were going to arrest me you wouldn't have come here alone."

"Not necessarily."

"What are you here for? What is this?"

"Remember that day at the courthouse when I told you I was going to lock you up?"

"Get to the point."

"I've been doing some thinking about that," Novak said. "I said to myself, 'What good is it to put someone in jail who might be able to do me some good?'"

Parisi came from behind the bar, sat down on a bar stool, adjusted his robe. "So maybe there is something that can be done?" he said in a conspiratorial tone.

"That's what I'm here to talk about."

"You're saying that maybe there is...uh...another way out?" Parisi wiped his chin, looked at his palm.

"That's what I'm saying."

"Now we're talking the same language," Parisi said.

"Both of us are part of this town," Novak said. "We live here. There's no reason why we can't work together."

"You wearing a wire?"

Novak shrugged off his coat, turned his palms upward. Parisi walked around him to inspect. "I came here
to talk man-to-man," Novak said.

Parisi nodded. "Let's get down to the bottom line."

Novak stepped to the wall stereo unit near the bar. He
reached into his pocket, removed a cassette tape,
shoved it in the tape port, turned up the volume. There
was the sound of a telephone ringing, Parisi answering
the telephone. It was a recording of the call Elliot had
made from the pay phone. Parisi swallowed a couple of
times as he listened. Color left his face.

After a minute, Novak turned off the tape player. "The
tape would kill you in court," he said.

Parisi moved to the bar again, mixed a drink, sipped.
"So you're here to shake down Tony Parisi."

Novak nodded.

"How much are you talking about?"

"A lot."

"Throw me a number," Parisi said.

"Fifteen."

Parisi thought for a moment. "How do you want it?"

"How do I want it?"

"The fifteen grand. You want it as a loan from a bank,
in cash, gold coins? You tell me."

Parisi's eyes followed Novak as he walked to the curtain, pulled the drape cord, revealed the Las Vegas sky-
line: desert sun coming alive behind air-conditioned
hotel/casinos. "I meant fifteen years in the joint, as op-
posed to five if you agree to testify before a federal
grand jury about all your connections in Las Vegas."

"You came here to blackmail me into becoming a stool
pigeon."

"I came here to give you an opportunity to cooperate
with the government," Novak said.

Parisi glared. "I want to talk to my attorney."

"You can call him from the federal lockup. You're
under arrest."

Parisi didn't move from where he was standing. He
sipped his drink. "Get out of here," he said with a nod
toward the door.

Novak sprang, yanked Parisi over the bar counter, slammed him to the floor. Parisi moaned as Novak twisted his arm behind him into a hammerlock, ratcheted handcuffs onto his wrists. Novak dragged him to his feet roughly, pulled him out of the room by his collar.

Parisi was still dressed only in his bathrobe when Novak marched him through the lobby past the crap and blackjack tables and out the front door.

 **33** A month later, a retirement party for Along-for-the-Ride Frank Tyde was held at Tyde's favorite restaurant, a German eatery which served stale beer and food John Novak considered inedible. The large banquet room was filled with federal and local law-enforcement officers and their wives. Tyde, wearing a novelty bow tie, was sitting at the head table flanked by supervisors from every police agency in town.

Novak sat at a table near the back with Red and Martha Haynes.

The new attorney-in-charge of the Las Vegas office of the Organized Crime Strike Force, a spindly man who Novak knew had never even met Tyde before he arrived in Las Vegas to take over the prosecution of Elliot and Parisi, finished giving a maudlin testimonial citing

Tyde's selfless and dedicated work on the Parisi case. The crowd applauded. He presented Tyde with the standard government retirement plaque and a large cartoon of Tyde asleep with his feet up on a desk. More applause.

"Can you imagine your taxes paying that jerk's pension for the rest of his life?" Haynes said without any attempt to lower his voice.

"Red," Martha Haynes said reproachfully.

Novak chuckled.

The attorney-in-charge introduced the Las Vegas sheriff, a bloated, red-faced man, who proceeded to tell off-color jokes. Everyone laughed.

Lorraine Traynor returned to Novak's table with two drinks. She set them on the table and sat down next to Novak. "I thought we'd need these to make it through the rest of the speeches," she whispered.

"Thanks for coming with me tonight," Novak whispered back.

"It's about time people got used to seeing us together," she said. Novak kissed her.

She put her hand in his. "But you are hereby ordered not to come to my chambers during the day."

"Yes, your honor."

It was the middle of the day in West Palm Beach. The ocean was whitecapped, rolling, and a steady breeze forced the trees along the strand to sway gently. Eddie Sands admired the scenery through the shaded glass that separated the restaurant from the beach.

The interior of the place was white latticework, starched table coverings, greenery and flowers. Waiters with French accents flitted among affluent diners dressed in the latest tropical clothing. The conversations that could be overheard involved nothing more pressing than whether dessert should be ordered from the pastry cart or the cheese-and-fruit tray.

As he lifted his wineglass, it occurred to him that though he and Monica were dressed properly in the latest designer fashion, they were probably the only ones in the place without deep cocoa tans. "Here's to our new home," he said.

"Courtesy of Uncle Sam's witness protection program," she whispered back.

Their wineglasses touched. They sipped. The gray-haired man and woman sitting at the next table looked at them and smiled. They smiled back.

A well-groomed waiter came to the table, carefully set plates in front of them: veal smothered with porcini mushroom sauce, baby carrots, and turnips. He moved away.

Monica made eye contact with the woman at the next table. "It's our first anniversary," she said.

"Congratulations."

"Thanks."

"Just visiting Palm Beach?" the woman asked.

"We came here to take time off and relax, but now we're getting anxious to do something," Monica said.

"We know how that is," the woman said. "What sort of work are you in?"

"I'm in investments...offshore banking," Monica said.

Sands offered his hand to the man. "Permit me to introduce myself. Edward Poindexter...my wife, Monica."

They shook hands, and the man introduced himself and his wife. "Welcome to Palm Beach," he said.

"I'm in investigation and security," Eddie Sands said.

"That must be an interesting line of work. Very hush-hush," the man said.

"It's certainly a challenge," Sands said.

The man wiped his mouth with a linen napkin. "How does one find oneself in such a profession?" he said.

"I was an FBI agent for twelve years."

"I see."

Eddie Sands reached into his shirt pocket, took out a business card, handed it to the man. "I specialize in handling private, sensitive matters," he said as the man examined the card. "Those requiring complete confidentiality." He smiled disarmingly.

The cocoa-tanned couple smiled back.